Christmas Honeymoon (For One)

A SWEET PARADISE RESORT CHRISTMAS NOVELLA

HOPE AUGUST

HOPE AUGUST INC

Hope August Inc
Cedar Park, TX

Cover Design by James, GoOnWrite.com

ISBN: 978-1-960048-01-1 (ebook)
ISBN: 978-1-960048-04-2 (print)
ISBN: 978-1-960048-10-3 (audiobook)

Newsletter

Let's stay in touch! Sign up for my newsletter at www.hopeaugust.com. Get early access to new releases, limited-time giveaways, and more.

Chapter One

"Ma'am, I *need* you to step aside." The customer service agent spoke as if she were talking to a child instead of a twenty-eight-year-old.

Kate shot the woman an apologetic smile as she continued digging through her purse. Crumpled receipts, a roll of mints, keys, and various other items she'd pulled out lay on the ticket counter for everyone to see. The chorus of sighs and grunts from behind her had become more noticeable, and her face burned with embarrassment.

"If you'll just give me another second," Kate muttered. She'd already spent several minutes holding up the line, but her ID had to be in her purse somewhere. She'd used it at the security checkpoint, for heaven's sake. "I *know* it's here."

A quick look over her shoulder confirmed that the line had doubled. Her eyes landed on the shoe tapping behind her and lifted until she stared into an unfamiliar face. With dark eyes and nostrils flaring, the man behind her released an exaggerated sigh. Blush deepening, she spun around to face the agent again. She didn't have time to worry about that egotistical jerk.

She literally couldn't afford to miss the flight. There was no such thing as a revenge vacation without taking the actual vacation. She had to check in to Sweet Paradise Resort by three in the afternoon, or she risked losing *all* the money she'd used to prepay for what should have been her snow-filled honeymoon. She still had hopes of getting a partial refund if she could just show up and explain to management what had happened.

Kate's heartbeat pounded in her ears as she mentally retraced her steps. Long-term parking. Bathroom. Coffee shop. That was it! She'd pulled it out when she bought her peppermint mocha. They were probably waiting for her to come back to claim it.

"*Ma'am*, I need you to move your belongings so I can help the next passenger—now." She lifted a perfectly arched brow and pursed her lips until more lines formed.

So much for friendly skies.

Kate swiped the items off the counter and into her purse then slipped the strap over her shoulder. She snatched her phone and gripped it tightly in her hands. *Please work.* Holding her thumb over the power button, she held her breath until it lit up and turned on. But just like earlier, the screen darkened before she could even open the airline app. *What a malfunctioning piece of junk.*

She hit the phone on her palm and groaned. Retrieving her e-boarding pass wouldn't do her any good anyway. She still needed her government-issued ID to board the plane. Her phone slipped from her fingers and landed on the floor next to a pair of dress shoes. She let out another garbled groan then dropped to retrieve the phone. Feeling Mr. Tapper's eyes on her, she lifted her gaze only to find his full of pity.

Kate scowled at him before glancing at her watch. *Shoot.* They would be boarding any minute. She slipped between the man and the counter to retrieve her suitcase and turned the way she'd come to head for the coffee shop. The wheels of her luggage bumped against something, but she had more important things to worry about. If she hurried, she'd make it back before the gates to the plane closed.

Beads of sweat dotted her brow, turning cold as she passed through the security checkpoint. All three lanes extended around the corner. How was she going to get through it again in time?

The cashier at the coffee shop must have seen her coming. She held up Kate's ID and smiled. "Looking for this?"

Kate snatched the ID. "Thanks," she said breathlessly. Her face was probably bright red, and she looked awful, but she didn't have time to say much more. She gave a little wave and sprinted back toward the checkpoint.

Hot tears of humiliation threatened to escape. *Don't cry. Don't cry.* Just because her ex-fiancé had left her for his coworker and today was going horribly and ridiculously wrong didn't mean she'd give in. She'd shed enough tears over that miserable excuse for a human being.

Kate took a deep breath and pushed forward. She'd get a printed ticket then attempt to get through security as quickly as possible. If she was lucky, she'd make it. She just needed *one* good thing to happen today.

She sprinted back to the other side of the airport, only to find the ticket counter line twice as long as the other one. The heavens opened and smiled on her when she saw two more agents open their counters, and the line moved forward.

"Looks like you're having a rough morning." The perky blonde grinned at her.

"You don't know the half of it," Kate puffed with a faint smile. "I just hope I make it to my gate before it's too late." She leaned on the counter, her breathing still heavy. "Is there any way I can request an aisle seat?"

The agent offered a sympathetic "Sorry, hon. This flight is

fully booked, and the rest of the seats are first come, first serve." The agent handed her a printed boarding pass and returned her ID. "You better hurry. They've just started boarding."

Kate's shoulders fell so low that her purse slid down her arm. "There's no way I'm going to make it through security," she mumbled.

The agent leaned forward and tapped Kate's ticket. "You were approved for TSA precheck."

Kate's eyes dropped to her ticket then bounced up to meet the agent's.

"Gate 5 is that way." She pointed to the left. "Better get going. And I hope your day gets better!"

Kate mouthed, "Thank you," then she scrambled for the TSA checkpoint. She was two gates away when the final call for her flight echoed over the loudspeaker.

"I'm here! I'm here!" Kate thrust the ticket at the uniformed woman standing near the gate. "*Please*. I have to make this flight," Kate wheezed between sucking in deep breaths.

The airline employee scanned the ticket before returning it to her. "Hurry up and find your seat."

Kate's carry-on luggage bounced off a few elbows before she stopped cold.

No. Not *him*.

When she'd finally thought things were looking up, she was proven wrong once again. Mr. Tapper sat in the seat beside the only empty one left on the plane. He'd taken the aisle seat, and now he had the nerve to pretend to be asleep. Didn't the flight crew announce that this would be a full flight? He had to know someone would be claiming the middle seat and he'd have to stand to let the person in.

Kate cleared her throat. "Excuse me."

His eyes flew open and met hers.

"I believe that's my seat." She pointed to the seat beside him.

His piercing jade-green eyes met her scowl. He stared at her blankly as if he hadn't heard a word she'd said. Then the corners of his lips twitched, rising into a crooked grin. His long lashes fluttered as he blinked at her, and the irritation in her chest eased. This was going to be an interesting flight.

Chapter Two

I t was her, the poor woman people were still whispering about when he boarded the plane. Liam attempted to bite back the smile that crossed his face. *What are the odds?* He shifted to get to his feet.

Thunk.

His hand flew to his head as a sharp pain sliced through his skull.

"Oh my gosh! I'm so sorry," she said. "Are you okay?"

Liam grimaced as he met the woman's eyes. Her cheeks were an adorable shade of red, making her blue eyes more prominent. She stared at him, not moving.

"Miss, we're about to pull away from the gate. You need to get into your seat."

They both turned toward the source of the voice and found a young flight attendant standing in the aisle.

Liam turned to grab her luggage and placed it in the overhead bin without preamble. The woman muttered her thanks and ducked into her seat. Her hands fluttered around her face, patting at her hair then tucking a few wayward strands behind her ear.

She buckled her seat belt then clutched her hands tightly in her lap.

Liam took his seat and leaned his head back. Closing his eyes, he pushed away the ache that plagued him. Sarah should have been here with him, sitting beside him and squeezing his hand when the plane took off. Instead, he was here only because it had been her dying wish.

He took a deep breath and counted down from ten. This trip was in her honor. She'd hate it if she knew he was moping.

"Business or pleasure?" The man sitting in the window seat leered at the woman between them.

She stiffened. "Pardon?"

His smile widened, and he ran a hand through greasy hair. "I'm visiting Colorado on business." He leaned closer to her, and his voice lowered slightly. "How about you?"

The woman's smile was forced, respectful. "Pleasure."

"That sounds right nice. I don't suppose you'd have time in your schedule for—"

Liam leaned forward. He reached for the woman's hand, causing her to jump.

The man's smile faltered as his eyes immediately dropped to the gesture.

Liam flashed him a smile. "Our apologies, sir. But my fiancée had a long morning. She's too nice to tell you, of course, but she'd like to rest for the trip."

Disappointment flickered across the man's features, and he straightened in his seat. "Of course."

Liam released the woman's hand and settled back into his chair. He felt her eyes boring into the side of his face even as the plane picked up speed and rose into the air. His stomach flipped each time the plane rose and leveled out.

A smile touched his lips. "You don't have to thank me," he whispered. "Just try not to injure me anymore." He peeked at her.

She gasped, and that lovely blush kissed her cheeks once more. She folded her arms and settled back into her seat, closing her eyes tightly. Despite her frazzled nature, she was quite attractive. Her bone structure was comparable to Sarah's, but that was where the similarities ended. Her nose was small, and her brows were darker than her hair. When her skin wasn't flushed, it was almost a light-caramel color. And if he wasn't careful, she'd open her eyes and find him staring.

He faced forward and allowed his mind to drift to the life he now had. Now that Sarah had been gone for six months, it was like everyone agreed he needed to move on. But what if he didn't want to? She'd been the love of his life. Living, breathing even, without her was nearly impossible. And now his friend Tyson wanted him to return from this trip to go on a blind date with his wife's coworker.

Nope. That wasn't going to happen. Only Tyson didn't believe him. The poor woman he'd set Liam up with had already started texting him about their plans after the new year.

He tightened his jaw. Why couldn't anyone see he wasn't ready to move on? Not now. Possibly not ever. Everyone thought this trip was about him letting go. Well, that was the last thing he planned on doing. He was going on this trip to feel closer to her. Not to forget her. They would see. They would *all* see that there was no one else for him.

He closed his eyes, and Sarah's smiling face filled his mind, easing the ache he carried. Sleep would come soon, and he'd feel a degree of peace.

Something tight and hard grabbed his hand, and his eyes shot open. The plane was rumbling, bumping from the turbulence as it descended in Colorado. Liam's gaze flew to his hand, finding the woman clutching it tightly enough that his fingers had turned white.

Her eyes were wide, and her face was almost as pale as his fingers had become.

"You okay?"

She yelped and stared at him. "What?"

He gestured to his hand. "You're cutting off the circulation to my hand."

A gasp escaped her lips, and she yanked her hand away. "Sorry."

Liam chuckled. "Don't like flying much, do you?"

"Don't make fun of me," she muttered. "Not everyone likes flying." They went over another bump, and she sucked in sharply.

"I wasn't making fun—" He shook his head. "Never mind. It was nice meeting you."

The wheels of the plane touched the ground, and he could see the relief wash over her. She glanced at him and opened her mouth but seemed to think better of speaking. Instead, she unbuckled her seatbelt with trembling hands.

"I think you're supposed to stay buckled until—" He shook his head again. *Whatever.* It wasn't like he'd be seeing her again. She could do what she wanted.

The plane came to a stop, and the pilot's voice sounded over the intercom system. "Ladies and gentlemen, we've arrived in Denver. The temperature is thirty-eight degrees. It's beginning to snow, so travel with care. Welcome to Colorado."

Waves of people got to their feet and immediately reached for their luggage. Liam stood and took a step back, allowing the woman to get into the aisle and away from the greasy man she'd been sitting beside.

He glanced down the aisle toward the back and was whacked against the head again. Grunting, he turned to the source and found the woman staring at him, her eyes as large as saucers and a look of shock on her face.

"I'm *so* sorry."

His eyes narrowed. "Well, third time's the charm, I suppose."

"Third time?" She shook her head. "I never—"

"Lady, it's your turn to go," a sharp voice behind him snapped.

Liam spun around and scowled at the young man. "Chill out, buddy. You'll get off the plane soon enough." He turned to face the woman, but she was already near the front of the plane. She glanced back at him for only a moment then disappeared as she disembarked.

"Trouble in paradise?" The man from the window seat sneered. "Looks like your woman might want some other company this trip, after all."

Liam clenched his hand into a fist then released it. The man wasn't worth his time. Liam yanked his duffel from the overhead compartment and headed down the aisle. None of this would matter once he made it to the resort. He had to focus on why he was here in the first place.

Chapter Three

ariah Carey's "All I Want for Christmas is You"
played over the loudspeakers, a heavy reminder
that Christmas was only four weeks away. Kate
passed several fake trees lit with white sparking lights. She shot
a look at her watch. The resort said there was a bus that would
pick up any guests. Unfortunately, the final bus would leave in
five minutes, and she'd arrived at the gate farthest from the
airport's exit. There was no way she'd make it.

Kate slowed enough to kick her heels off and slip them
into her purse before running down the aisle between the
gates. Several passengers heading in her direction called out in
frustration as she muttered her apologies and bumped into
one person and then another.

Her face burned with embarrassment. If her phone was
working, she would be able to get an Uber. Taxis were not an
option with the tight budget she was on. At this point, the bus
was her only option, and missing it might mean she'd be late
to check-in.

*Why did I agree to come? This whole thing was a giant
mistake.* She got stuck behind a huge group of tourists that

blocked the escalators. They argued about where they needed to go for a rental car. She stood on her toes and attempted to get through them, but they ignored her.

Kate let out a groan and headed for the cascading stairs to the side. She reached the automatic doors, huffing and puffing, hunched over, with an ache in her side. Pushing through, she swiveled her head to the right and then the left. *Where is it? The bus has to be here somewhere.*

Kate glanced at her watch. She'd made it just in time. Scurrying down the long-paved sidewalk, she approached an airline attendant. "Excuse me. I'm looking for the bus that goes to the Sweet Paradise Resort."

The man leaned forward over his desk and pointed the way she'd come. A bright-red bus on the second lane of traffic chuffed forward, spurting exhaust in its wake. "No, no, no, no!" She ran toward it helplessly. Finding another way meant she'd have to spend money she didn't have.

Her shoulders drooped, causing the strap of her purse to slide down her arm. Kate heaved a heavy sigh. This whole trip had been a huge mistake. Coming here had been her friend's bright idea, not her own. She should just go home and cut her losses. She would be miserable if she stayed anyway.

Kate pulled out her phone and sent a little prayer heavenward. *Please work.* By some miracle, the phone's screen lit up. She let out a squeal and quickly made a phone call.

Ansley answered on the first ring. "Did you make it? Are you snuggled up next to a giant fireplace as the snow falls outside the window, reading that romance book I got you?"

Kate bit her lower lip. "Not exactly."

"Well, have you met any cute guys? I'm sure there are plenty there."

"Ansley, the men who will be at that resort are going to be with fiancées and spouses. I'm going to be the only single one there." She shook her head. "Actually, I won't. I need you to change the flight home."

"What? No. I'm not letting you come home yet. You need this."

"Look, I appreciate that you bought my airline tickets, but I really shouldn't have come. Only a crazy person would come on their honeymoon after their fiancé chose another woman."

"Or a genius one. Sweetie, what's going on? We talked about this. You already spent the money on the trip. It's non-refundable. You even scheduled the time off."

Kate moved out of the way of a large family and offered them an apologetic smile. "It's just been one thing after another. I lost my ID. I sat next to this sleazeball of a guy on the plane, and now I missed my ride."

"So, get a taxi or an Uber."

She sighed. "I can't afford that right now. I barely have any money in my bank account as it is. I spent almost all my savings on that wedding." Her chest tightened, making it hard to breathe. "Just call the airline since the confirmation is in your name and have the flight changed."

"I can't do that."

"Why not?"

"I'm decorating my Christmas tree. What do you think? Color or white?"

"*Ansley.*"

Her friend sighed. "If it comes down to it, *I'll* schedule you an Uber. Hold on. I just have to figure out—"

"Ansley? Hello?" Kate pulled her phone away and stared at it. The screen was once again dark. *Dang it!* She pushed the power button, but nothing happened. "Work. Just do what you were meant to do and *work.*"

Someone bumped into her, causing her to lose her grip on the phone. The device slipped to the concrete with a sickening thwack, landing facedown. Disheartened, Kate stared at it.

The idiot who'd collided with her arm didn't even stop to apologize.

Closing her eyes, she counted, *One... two... three...*

When she opened them, she had to stifle the screech that sat on the tip of her tongue.

The man from the plane stood in front of her. He cocked his head to the side as he held out her sorry excuse for a phone on the palm of his hand. "Is this yours?"

Her cheeks filled with heat as she snatched the phone from him. "Yes," she mumbled, her gaze dropping to her cracked screen. "Thank you."

His lips twitched at the corners. "I hope you have a better day." He turned toward the road and shifted his attention to his phone.

"Excuse me, ma'am. That bus for the Sweet Paradise Resort said they can send one more out here to pick you up." Out of nowhere, the flight attendant appeared at her side. "If you'd like me to have them—"

"Sweet Paradise Resort?" The man turned toward her again. "Are you staying there?"

Kate tucked a lock of hair behind her ear, her face still flushed. "Yes." She turned to the attendant. "Really? They'd be able to do that?" Maybe it was a sign. She was supposed to be here.

"That won't be necessary," the man from the flight interrupted. "I'm grabbing an Uber. You can share my ride."

Her head whipped around, and she gaped at him. "What? No. You don't have to do that."

He flashed her a smile and waved off the attendant. "It's not a big deal. It costs the same for me either way." He held out his hand. "I'm Liam. And you are?"

"Kate," she muttered, glancing toward the retreating attendant as if he'd be able to save her from this embarrassing never-ending story.

The man chuckled. "Relax. I don't bite."

A car pulled up, and the driver got out. "You Liam?"

Liam nodded and jerked his thumb over his shoulder toward Kate. "There's two of us."

Kate opened her mouth to argue then thought better of it. The resort was just a short ride up the mountain. She adjusted the strap of her purse and strode toward the car. The driver took her suitcase and placed it in the trunk beside Liam's. When she turned, Liam was holding the door open for her.

"Thanks," she mumbled and ducked inside.

Liam climbed in after her.

The driver returned to his seat and glanced back at them. "We're waiting for another couple and then we can go." His focus bounced from Kate to Liam. "How long have you two been together?"

Kate let out a bark of laughter, causing Liam to shoot her a sharp look. She clasped her hand over her mouth. "Sorry, we're not together."

Liam stared at her for a full, unnerving minute before he met the driver's gaze. "She's right. I tend to shy away from abusive relationships."

Kate gasped and stared at him wide-eyed. "I never—"

He chuckled, gesturing toward her as he continued. "This one not only rolled over my foot with her suitcase, but she hit me in the head with it too. Twice."

If it was possible, the flush in her face deepened even further. She wouldn't have been surprised if she resembled a pomegranate rather than a human at this point. Okay, this ride wasn't lucky. It was part of the curse she'd been experiencing for the last three months.

Chapter Four

T he Uber driver pulled up in front of a large five-story building framed by equally elegant smaller struc-tures. Exterior lights gave a golden hue to the pale-brown brick, and a towering evergreen tree twinkling with Christmas lights rose above the nearby shrubs and a small white picket fence. Everything glittered as dusk fell around the main building. Fluffy white flakes danced lazily on a gentle breeze, adding to the whole picture. It was almost like Liam had been transported through time and space to a magical wonderland. This place was truly paradise.

Liam pushed open the door and stepped out into the cold evening. He held out his hand to Kate, who took one look at his offering and dismissed it. Her eyes didn't even meet his as she scrambled from the vehicle, murmuring, "Thanks for the ride," then hurried around to the trunk.

He watched as she headed inside. Part of him itched to pull her aside and ask her what was wrong. She was obviously struggling with something. The other, more logical part of him knew he needed to just let things be. Her reason for being at the resort, whatever it was, wasn't his business. It wasn't like he would be sharing all the sordid details for why he was there either.

Liam offered the driver a thankful nod as he grabbed his luggage. He made it to the reception desk and stood right behind Kate. She peeked at him over her shoulder then stiffened when he flashed her a smile.

"Next," the man behind the counter smiled warmly. "Welcome to Sweet Paradise Resort. Are you here for the couples retreat?"

Liam straightened. *She's here with someone?* An odd twinge of disappointment snaked through him. From the moment he'd arrived in Colorado, all he'd been able to think about was how he should have been there with Sarah. Now this woman had managed to turn everything inside out.

The host behind the counter gestured toward him. "And your husband? Will he need—"

Liam stiffened, and his gaze bounced to the woman in front of him.

She hunched down, her hand coming to her forehead. "No. He's not my—I'm not with him."

Confusion flickered across the man's features. "My apologies." He peered at the computer screen. "Will Mr. Scott be arriving later today or—"

"I'm here *alone*," she muttered. "Actually, can I speak with your manager? I've been trying to reach someone in management for the past month, but—"

The gentleman frowned. "I'm sorry. We've been short-staffed, and it can be difficult to return the numerous calls we get."

"It's fine. I just want to speak to a manager."

"He's gone for the day, but he'll be back tomorrow."

She shook her head. "It's important. I want to change my reservation. I don't want to participate in the couples activities. I understand the room can't be refunded, but all the extras—" She squirmed and glanced at Liam again, her face red.

Something was wrong, and the dull ache in his chest intensified. That must be why he was drawn to her. They had something in common. They were both here without the person they loved.

"I'm terribly sorry, miss, but the retreat is also non-refundable."

Her shoulders slumped. He took a step forward, prepared to help her plead her case, but then the man continued.

"But..." The man flashed her a smile and leaned forward. "This week, I hear they're doing a raffle."

She lifted her head.

"Every activity will get a certain number of entries, and the hotel will refund the stay and the retreat fees for one lucky couple. Of course, seeing as you're here alone... that might be difficult. Some of the activities require you to be in a partnership." He gave her an apologetic look.

"Really?" The hope that dripped from the tone of her voice was almost pitiful. At least she had something to look forward to. "I guess it's better than nothing."

Liam glanced around the lobby as she continued her check-in. There had to be several couples here for the retreat. He had signed up before Sarah received her diagnosis. Life wasn't fair, and he knew first-hand how hard it could be to bounce back from something devastating. He got the feeling this woman needed a win.

He shifted his weight from one foot to the other. It was rude to eavesdrop. From the sound of it, she'd suffered enough; she didn't need spectators. His phone buzzed, and he pulled it out of his back pocket. Stifling the urge to groan, he slid his thumb across the screen and read the message from Tyson.

Tyson: *Hey bro. Rebecca is on board. I gave her your number.*

Liam shook his head and clicked on the message. He'd lost count of all the times he'd told Tyson no. He wasn't ready to date anyone just yet.

Liam: *Dude! Why did you do that? I told you no dates.*

The little bubble popped up, indicating Tyson was typing something. Then it disappeared. Liam let out a harsh sigh.

Liam: *I mean it! NO dates.*

"Next!"

His head popped up. The woman was gone, and the host waved him over. After five minutes of being checked in and listening to reminders that he had been assigned to a room without a television or Wi-Fi due to the nature of his visit, he headed for the elevators. Initially, it had sounded romantic that the hotel promoted more togetherness by taking away modern distractions. Now, it would make for a very lonely week.

He glanced down at his phone once more to confirm Tyson hadn't messaged him back. Liam cared for his friend, but the guy was an idiot. Couldn't he tell that Liam was still grieving the death of his fiancée?

Liam rounded the corner to the elevators just as they started to close. He sprinted forward and shoved his arm between the doors just in time. When they opened, they revealed the woman from earlier.

He let out a chuckle. "We have to stop running into each other like this."

She dropped her gaze, and her light-brown hair fell like a waterfall, hiding her face.

Liam took his place beside her, glancing at the lit buttons on the control panel. Fourth floor. They were headed to the same place. He leaned against the wall and shifted his focus to her again. He opened his mouth, then his phone vibrated again.

Tyson: *I'm not canceling. You need this. It's time to move on. Sarah's dead. She'd want you to be happy.*

He ticked his jaw back and forth. Yes, Sarah was dead. And he'd been madly in love with her. This trip wasn't because he couldn't let go. They'd planned this trip together, and she'd made him promise her that he wouldn't bail. If Tyson knew that little detail, he'd only push Liam harder to go on this date with Rebecca. What if Liam didn't want to move on? What if he wanted to cling to the last bit of Sarah's memory he could?

He shoved the phone into his pocket. Messaging Tyson would only feed the anger swirling in his stomach. They couldn't see eye-to-eye on this subject, and they never would. Tyson had never lost anyone close to him.

The elevator doors slid open, and the woman darted through them like she couldn't stand to share the same air he breathed. That was just as well; it wasn't like he wanted to spend any quality time with anyone either. He was there as a promise to his lost love. By the end of the week, he would be able to complete his mission, and then maybe he would consider listening to Tyson. But at this point, the probability was slim.

Adjusting his duffel strap, he ducked out into the hallway and headed down the corridor toward his room. Tomorrow was the first day of the retreat. From what he could remember, the first activity was a tour of the mountain via snowmobile. At least that should be fun.

Chapter Five

Kate took in a deep breath and let it out her nose with measured patience. The breath showed up like a white puff of smoke. She must look just like a fire-breathing dragon. "Like I said, I don't have a partner. I came alone." She stood in front of the woman in charge of the snowmobile tour while several couples were obviously eavesdropping on her conversation. She was certain she could feel their eyes on her, judging her.

The woman's brows furrowed, and her voice stumbled over her next statement. "But it says on my paperwork that you signed up with a Mr.—"

Kate placed her mittened hand on her clipboard and spoke through gritted teeth. "You'll forgive me for coming by myself when the person on that list is an unfaithful—" She bit back the words that threatened to escape her lips. "It doesn't matter," she clipped. "I was told there would be the opportunity to win a refund for this retreat, but I have to participate. So let me do this. I am more than capable of driving a snowmobile."

She shifted, and her eyes darted to the group of waiting

couples. They'd been outside long enough that everyone's cheeks and noses had turned red from the cold. With each passing minute, she seemed to be getting more anxious. "I'm sorry, ma'am. But according to the rules of the couples retreat raffle, this activity requires you to be part of a couple. We don't want there to be an unfair advantage."

"*Unfair*—" She shook her head. "If anything, my being on my own would give *others* the advantage."

"Not necessarily. Some of these activities are teambuilding exercises where you have to work together." The attendant hugged her clipboard to her chest. "Didn't the host at check-in tell you this? I'm just supposed to get you guys up the mountain."

Really? She wasn't going to budge on this.

Kate let out a groan. "He may have mentioned some-thing." This was exactly how everything was going to end—by her walking away empty-handed. No money, no husband... nothing. "But no one gave me a list of which activities I can do by my—"

"Sorry I'm late. I slept through my alarm."

Kate's whole body tensed at the familiar voice. *No. Please don't be him. Anyone but him.*

The woman in front of her lifted her gaze and flashed whoever it was a smile. "You're right on time. What's your name?"

"Liam. Liam Harper."

If it was possible, the woman's smile widened further. "Ah, yes. You and Miss Anderson are on my list." Her gaze shifted, looking out over the other guests before returning to Liam's face. "Where is Miss Anderson?"

Liam cleared his throat. "She was unable to attend."

The woman's features brightened even more. She was practically a lit tree. Her gaze bounced to Kate, whose gaze widened. Kate held up both hands, shaking her head vehemently.

She gestured to Kate. "Miss Lloyd is without a partner as well. The two of you can couple up."

The silence was almost palpable.

Kate could feel his eyes boring into the back of her head. She shook her head again. "No, that isn't—"

"No, I don't think—"

The woman's focus bounced from Kate to Liam and back as they spoke up at the exact same moment. Her features seemed tight as she glanced down at her clipboard again.

Several whispers from the couples who surrounded them seemed to swarm her. This was none of their business. If they knew what she was going through, they wouldn't be paying her any mind. The attendant picked up a sheet of paper to read the document beneath it then brought her attention to Kate again. She took a step toward her and lowered her voice.

"Miss Lloyd, I understand you don't want to be here. I have a note that states you have already requested a refund. My job is to make sure everyone enjoys their time today. I can't give you a refund, but I can tell you that if you participate with Mr. Harper, then you have a better shot at getting exactly what you need."

Kate folded her arms tightly over her chest. "This is a *couples* retreat. I'm not going to partner up with a stranger."

It was like the whispers had continued to grow, encircling her head, yelling at her. Kate closed her eyes to shut them out, forcing her blush to stay hidden deep beneath her skin. This had to be the most mortifying thing she'd ever been part of.

The woman glanced in Liam's direction. She gave them a pleading look. "Please. This is my first day. I just want to get everything off on the right foot. We're already behind schedule. Do you think you can agree just for today? Then I can see what I can do to help you after?"

Kate shot Liam a look over her shoulder. His dark-green eyes seemed less severe today. They were soft, almost warm. Maybe he'd gotten a good night's sleep. Her breath hitched in her throat, and she whipped her head back to meet the woman's gaze. "Fine. I'll do it if he does."

The attendant shifted her focus to Liam. Silence that probably only took a few seconds seemed to last for several minutes. Kate's heart beat a little faster, and her whole body itched. Why did she suddenly feel like she was waiting for her first prom date to pick her up, wondering if he was going to bail on her?

"Fine," he mumbled. His lack of excitement was almost disappointing. Almost.

Relief flickered across the attendant's face, and she smiled brightly at them. "Great! I'm sure you two will get along famously."

Kate snorted. "Sure."

Chapter Six

L iam stared at the back of Kate's head, wondering when she would finally look at him. Instead, she turned, her attention following the woman who had just convinced them to do the most ridiculous thing he'd ever heard of.

Why would it matter if they were on their own? Who cared if this was supposed to be a couples retreat? Just because the two of them had come separately didn't mean they needed to be paired up.

Whatever. He'd agreed, and now he had to deal with it. The attendant wandered through the group, telling everyone about the first activity. It was a tour via snowmobile. What more did they need to know?

"This is a trust exercise. One of you will be a passenger; the other will be the driver. And one of you will be blindfolded."

Several gasps and giggles filled the air.

The woman broke into it. "Don't worry. The passenger is going to be the blindfolded one. The last thing we need is for one of you to run straight into a tree."

Laughter erupted from the group.

"Each activity will give you an allotted number of entries for the raffle at the end of the week. The winning couple will get a full refund *and* another all-expenses paid trip next year." The woman knew how to hold an audience.

Liam's gaze shifted to Kate again. She fidgeted with her hands, still avoiding his gaze. He could tell she knew he was looking. She tried to hide it, but the way she was shifting made it clear.

His phone vibrated, and he pulled it out. Letting out a groan, he swiped open the screen to stare at the message from Rebecca. She was giving him her contact information because of Tyson. He groaned again. Hadn't he told his friend he didn't want anything to do with a setup? Tyson had gone against his wishes... again.

Liam pressed his thumb on the reply window. He should tell her he wasn't ready. He should explain that his friend was an idiot and apologize for him. Then, without knowing exactly why, he swiped out of the screen. One date wouldn't hurt, right?

When he looked up from his phone, the group was wandering toward a line of snowmobiles. *Shoot!* He shoved his phone into his pocket and grabbed his gloves. Pulling them on, he caught up to Kate.

"We have to stop meeting like this."

She gave him a strange look. "*Really?*"

"What?"

"*That's* the line you choose?"

He held up both hands and gave her a crooked smile. "I thought it would be funny."

She rolled her eyes as she continued to stomp through the snow.

Irritation swirled inside him. He hadn't agreed to couple with her because he wanted to spend time with her. He'd done it to help *her* out. "Hey, I didn't have to agree to this."

"So why did you?" Her voice was flat, unfeeling.

Why do the pretty ones all have an attitude? He jogged around to cut her off and set his steely stare on her. "Because I could tell you needed it more than I did."

Her angry expression faltered, and she looked away. "Oh."

Liam shoved his hands into his coat pockets. "We're going to be together for the next six days. We might as well get along so we can win you that refund."

Kate's eyes rose to meet his again. "Okay. Thanks."

Moving out of her way, he gestured toward the snowmobiles. "Let's see if we can get you some entries."

A ghost of a smile appeared on her lips. Dang, she was beautiful. Her large eyes paired with her small nose and the freckles sprinkled across its bridge were absolutely adorable. He shook off the thought. He wasn't here to find a girl. He was here to make good on the promise he'd made Sarah.

Kate picked up a helmet and situated herself on the snowmobile, leaving the space behind her empty.

"Oh no you don't." He wouldn't be caught dead blindfolded while a stranger drove them through the trails in the snow-covered mountains.

She glanced at him in surprise.

"Have you ever driven one of these?"

Kate shrugged. "It can't be *that* hard, can it?"

Liam shoved the blindfold toward her. "These are hard when you're driving by yourself. When you have more weight on the back, it gets even worse. I'm driving."

Her brows lowered, but she didn't argue. Instead, she snatched the blindfold and tied it on. He grabbed his helmet and sat on the seat in front of her. She slipped her arms around his waist, and his heart lurched into his throat. Her touch was soft, almost like a caress. It wouldn't take much to pretend Sarah was the one behind him.

No, he was getting better. He needed to stay grounded.

That was what Sarah would have wanted. Liam started the engine and revved it a little before darting forward. Kate's grip on him tightened, and she let out a sound that was a blend of a laugh and a squeal. "Don't you dare crash," she called over the engine. "Get us there safely."

"Oh, I'll do more than get us there safely, sweetheart. I'll make sure we win." Okay, so the activity wasn't about speed. But he couldn't deny how good it felt to experience human touch again. She rested her cheek between his shoulder blades. They wove through the trees behind the tour guide.

There were moments he could pick up the speed. Cold, biting air blasted his face. The wind whipped and tugged at his clothing. The thrill was exactly what he needed to get his mind off darker memories. He was breathing new life into his future without Sarah.

The whole group pulled off as they reached the crest of a hill overlooking the resort. Kate ripped off her blindfold and stared around wildly. Her breathing had quickened, and she had a pretty glow in her cheeks. "That was actually kinda fun."

Liam held out his hand, helping her from her seat. "It was, wasn't it?" He peeked at her as they wandered to where the others stood, taking pictures and gushing about the view. They stood there in silence for about fifteen minutes.

Then his curiosity got the better of him. Liam cleared his throat. "Can I ask you something?"

Without looking at him, she shrugged. "Sure."

"Where's Mr. Scott?"

She stiffened.

"I heard his name a few times," he hurried to admit. "You don't have to tell me if you don't want to."

Her jaw tightened, and her eyes lost the little bit of light they'd held. Dang it, he'd gone and been too nosy again.

"He broke up with me a few days before the wedding."

Liam sucked in a sharp breath. "I'm sorry," he murmured.

"It gets better." She eyed him. "Turns out he was more interested in a girl he worked with. I guess it's hard not to fall for someone you see every day."

Dang. No wonder she was in such a sour mood. He couldn't blame her at all. It made sense that she wanted her money back for this trip. He opened his mouth to tell her this Mr. Scott didn't deserve her, but the guide interrupted him.

"Mr. Harper, do you feel comfortable pulling up the rear? We're about to head back."

He nodded. "Right. Sure." He exchanged a look with Kate. The moment had passed. But they had almost a full week where he could make that point.

Snowmobiles started up, and the group started their way down the mountain. Together, he and Kate headed for their vehicle. Her arm shot out and gripped his forearm. "Liam," she whispered, "look!"

His gaze swiveled around until his eyes landed on a huge brown bull moose. The antlers had to be so long that if Liam were to stretch out both his arms as far as he could, he still couldn't reach both antler tips. The graceful creature was about thirty yards away, wandering up a frozen stream.

"Have you ever seen one of those in person?" Kate's whisper was full of awe. "I heard there are a few that travel down from the northern parts of Maine, but I've never seen them."

He dragged his attention from the moose to Kate. "You live in northern Maine?"

She nodded; her eyes still locked on the beast. "About twenty minutes outside of Presque Isle."

"I live about ten minutes away from Presque Isle."

Finally, she looked at him. "Really?"

He nodded. "Small world."

"Yeah, I guess." Her eyes drifted toward where their group

had gone. "Uh oh. We might lose them." She hurried toward their snowmobile and climbed on. "Come on. We have to hurry."

"Don't worry. We'll be fine." He sauntered over to the vehicle. "I have a great sense of direction."

Chapter Seven

"**D**on't worry? I didn't think your sense of direction would land our only mode of transportation directly into a ditch," Kate screeched.

"Relax. No one got hurt. It was only a small ditch. I'm sure they'll realize we didn't return and send a rescue team after us." Liam stood at the edge of the shallow ravine and stared at the snow mobile.

He was right. It wasn't that deep, but the way he'd managed to lodge the vehicle into the crevice made it impossible for the two of them to pull it loose.

Kate groaned and threw her hands down at her sides. "I can't believe I trusted you to get us back safe. I told you to take a right at the fork, but you didn't listen."

Liam spun around to face her, a scowl now prevalent on his face. "Who was the blindfolded rider when we came up?"

"Me," she murmured.

"Exactly. So just why do you think I would ever listen to you when it came to directions? Women are all alike," he muttered under his breath. "They think they know best when they really don't."

Her fury reignited. "Excuse me? Anyone with eyeballs could see there were tracks leading in the direction I told you to take."

He gestured wildly around them. "And there were tracks leading this way too. It was an honest mistake."

"It's a mistake that could end up getting us killed. What if that ravine had been deeper? Worse, what if it had been the edge of a cliff and not a ravine at all?" Her breathing had grown ragged. She'd about had it with his attitude. "From the second I met you, you've been nothing but impatient and arrogant. Why should I give you the benefit of the doubt when you haven't shown me any such courtesy?"

Liam's brows shot up but then immediately lowered over his eyes. His jaw clenched, and he took three swift steps through the snow toward her, causing her to take a step back. Her boot caught on a stone, throwing off her balance. Kate's eyes widened, and her arms flailed wildly. She sucked in a breath, bracing herself for contact with the frozen earth beneath her, but the impact never came.

Kate blinked rapidly and opened her eyes to find his jade eyes staring into hers. His face was so close, she could feel his warm, minty breath against her cold, chapped cheek.

"Are you okay?" he asked. The low timbre of his voice was like something out of a romance movie.

Knots in her stomach twisted for just a moment, and she nodded, her mouth too dry to speak.

He'd managed to slip his arm around her waist and used his weight to counterbalance her fall. Her gloved hands grasped tightly to his upper arms as if releasing him would surely land her on the ground with a bruised backside. Liam was too close. Especially considering the fight they'd just had. She wasn't in the right headspace for something like this.

Kate scrambled from his arms and tugged sharply on her coat, adjusting it back to where it was supposed to be. Her eyes remained on her boots. The anger had fizzled somewhat, but she was still on edge. First things first, though—how were they going to get back down the mountain without a vehicle to take them there? He was probably right. A search team would likely find them before matters got much worse, but that didn't make her feel any better. The last place she wanted to be was in the woods with a stranger.

When she lifted her gaze, Liam was back to the edge of the ravine. He had his hands on his hips as he stared at the source of their predicament.

"Unless you have some kind of super vision, I don't think staring at it is going to help us much."

He glanced at her over his shoulder. "Well, I don't see you doing anything to help the matter." Liam took a deep breath and let it out slowly. His voice softened. "Do you have your phone on you?"

She shook her head. "When they told us that phones were prohibited, I figured I'd rather be safe than sorry."

"Right. Me too."

A soft smile touched her lips. She hadn't taken him for the type to be a strict rule follower. It wasn't like anyone would have discovered it if he'd hidden the phone in his coat pocket. It was refreshing.

Knock it off. He's not your type. You don't even know if he has a girlfriend. Then again, if he had a girlfriend, why wouldn't she be on this couples retreat?

Kate's gaze trailed over Liam again. He was attractive. And he'd had a few moments where she could see why someone might be interested. But not her. She'd just gotten out of a poisonous relationship. The last thing she needed was to dive right in to another one—even if the guy had the most gorgeous green eyes she'd ever seen.

Liam turned, catching her staring. Kate's face warmed,

and she turned away. *Great. He probably thinks I have a crush on him. Guys like that usually have big heads.*

Well, lucky for them both, she didn't and wouldn't. In fact, the second they were rescued, she would insist they find someone new to pair her up with or figure out a loophole for their dumb rules regarding the competition. The organizers of this whole retreat had to give in now. Liam had practically put her life in danger.

Against her own volition, her gaze drifted over in his direction again. Why was he here without a date? She'd told him *her* story. Then again, asking him seemed like an invasion of privacy. If he hadn't offered that kind of information willingly, maybe his story was more painful than hers.

Her heart lurched at the thought. Though she could mope the rest of her life and claim all men were awful, there could be worse things than being left before the wedding day.

Kate shoved her hands into her pockets and trudged toward him. The snow crunched beneath her boots, making soft chuffing sounds that filled the quiet, frozen morning. She took in a deep breath, preparing to ask the hard questions, then the sound of several familiar engines surrounded them.

Liam straightened, and they both turned just as three snowmobiles leapt over a small hill.

Maybe it was fate. She probably shouldn't put her nose where it didn't belong. That didn't mean she wouldn't demand to speak with the head of this couples retreat. She needed to find a way out of this arrangement as soon as possible.

Chapter Eight

Okay, he'd screwed up. Liam could admit that. Their first outing was supposed to be a fun escape. Kate had needed that. Based on what she'd gone through with her ex-fiancé, Kate was probably the only one who needed this retreat more than anyone else there. Then he'd gone and wrecked their snowmobile.

He sat at the table in the ballroom of the hotel and reluctantly glanced in the direction of the banquet table. Kate was still arguing with their poor tour guide, no doubt demanding that they no longer be paired up. By the looks of those participating at this resort, there were no other options left for her. He fought the instinct to feel wounded by her demands. He wasn't all that bad. Sure, they didn't have the best track record since meeting, but there had been some good moments too—those quiet minutes they'd spent on the mountain and the moose. When he'd caught her staring, he'd thought they might have shared something.

But what was he thinking? She couldn't stand him. Kate was here for one reason and one reason only. She wanted her money back. If the resort could give that to her, she would have been long gone by now.

Liam, on the other hand, had a few more things he needed to do before he could call this trip done. He let out a sigh and ran his hand through his mussed hair. While they'd been on their little tour that morning, he'd gotten a message from Rebecca. She was looking forward to their date.

It'd be better if he could just clear his mind of everything going wrong in his life at the moment. His gaze trailed over the room. A real Christmas tree that had to be at least fifteen feet tall sat up against one corner. The white twinkling lights gave it a timeless look. Couple that with the red-and-gold glass ball ornaments, and it looked like it had been decorated for Times Square.

"Holly Jolly Christmas" played softly over the intercom system, and the smell of ham and potatoes mingled with the pine scent of the tree. *If Sarah was here, she would be all over this.* Liam thumped his elbow on the table and placed his chin in his hand. She would have hated his gloomy attitude.

He shot a look in Kate's direction once more. She looked absolutely stunning in a simple floor-length black dress that hugged her figure. This dinner was one of two formal evenings scheduled. Had he not messed up with their ride back, she might have been sitting with him at the table, instead of demanding a change. His thoughts drifted back to Rebecca. At least there was one woman who was interested in spending some time with him. He'd nearly canceled on her, but something had stopped him. He'd just given in, like he always did.

Turning toward the stage, he tuned in to what the host was saying. "We're all thrilled to welcome you to the official opening night of our couples retreat at Sweet Paradise Resort. I'm sure you all enjoyed the tour this morning and can't wait for what else we have planned. For now, sit back, relax, and let's do some karaoke."

Kate thumped into the seat beside him. They were the only ones at the table. It was as if all the other couples had found buddies and were thoroughly enjoying keeping their distance from the strange couple who wasn't a real couple.

Liam glanced at Kate's dismal expression. "No luck, I take it."

She shot him an irritated look out of the corner of her eye. "What are you talking about?"

"You were trying to get out of being my partner this week."

A groan escaped her lips as she placed her elbows on the table and dug her hands into her hair. "It's nothing personal. But this is a—"

"*Couples* retreat. And we're not a couple."

"*Exactly*. How do none of them get this? They charge us an arm and a leg with the promise of getting closer to our partner. Not only that, but I'm sure they put it in their brochure that they guarantee a love that grows exponentially over the course of the week." She lifted her head so she could meet his gaze. "No offense, but being in love is the last thing I want right now."

"None taken." He glanced at her again then faced her fully. Leaning forward, he lowered his voice. "Look, I feel like we got off on the wrong foot. I want to help you get what you came here for. Maybe we can start over?"

She considered him. Her eyes narrowed slightly before she shrugged and sat back in her chair. "Fine. I don't really have any other choice."

"Not really."

The band started playing an upbeat version of "Let It Snow" while an older couple belted out the lyrics horribly off-key. Kate's features softened somewhat as she watched them, and Liam couldn't help but stare at her. Her eyes seemed to sparkle, and her features were glowing.

"You like music, don't you?"

Kate jumped. "What?"

"Music." Liam gestured toward the couple on stage. "They're singing horribly, but there's something about it that you actually like."

The glow intensified, and she looked away from him. "I may or may not enjoy singing."

His brows lifted. "Are you any good?"

She let out a short laugh. "What kind of question is that?"

"Just curious." Sarah had been a singer. It was one of the things he loved about her, the way her voice could hit the note perfectly to bring a tear to a listener's eye. She was heaven incarnate.

Kate's eyes met his again. "I'm okay, I guess."

"You have to go up there."

Her eyes widened. "I don't sing in front of people."

"Why not?" He chuckled. "If you have a talent, you should share it."

"Because it's embarrassing."

Liam cocked his head to the side. "I'll go if you go. Besides, I think this is one of those events that gets you closer to that grand prize."

That seemed to stop her argument. A wicked little smile touched her lips, and she stood from her seat. "Deal." Faster than he expected, she strode around his chair, grabbed his hand, and tugged him toward the stage.

In a matter of seconds, she'd picked out a song, then they were standing under a set of very bright lights. He looked over at her bright eyes. Excitement was bursting from every part of her. This might be the stupidest thing he'd do all week, but the next few minutes would make it worth it.

The music for "Baby, It's Cold Outside" filled the room, and Kate brought her microphone to her lips. She hit every single note with perfection. Not only that, but she moved with the music like she was performing some kind of show.

His mouth dropped open. She wasn't just pretty good—she was amazing, like try-out-for-one-of-those-reality-TV-shows amazing.

Kate turned toward him, her eyes widening slightly. What did she want? She mouthed, "Your turn."

Liam jumped into action and faced the small computer screen that had been set up for their convenience. His performance came in severely lacking, but it didn't matter. The second the song was over, the whole crowd burst into applause.

Kate gave him another heart-stopping smile before the two of them hurried off the stage. When they managed to get to their table, he whirled around to face her and instinctively pulled her in for a bearhug. As he stood back, his words spilled from his lips excitedly. "*Pretty good*? Darling, you were incredible."

For a split second, she froze. Then she took a step back and shoved her hands behind her back. "Thanks." She looked over her shoulder toward the double doors. "I think I'm going to get some air."

His brows furrowed at her retreating form. She'd gone from warm and excited to shut off. Was it something he'd said? He went over the words he'd just said, then his stomach bottomed out. Dang his big mouth. He hadn't been thinking clearly. They'd both been on an adrenaline rush and right after they'd gotten to a friendly place.

He rose from his chair, grabbed his coat, and hurried after her.

Chapter Nine

The second Kate made it out onto the veranda, she regretted not snatching her coat from her seat in the ballroom. The air was colder than she remembered it being earlier in the day. Then again, she'd been wearing her coat.

Her face practically burned with all the compliments Liam had thrown at her. Either he was either very easily impressed, or he had some ulterior motives. It was possible he wanted the grand prize as much as she did.

He hadn't given her any details regarding why he was there alone. It didn't seem likely that he'd had a similar experience to her own. Otherwise, he would have shared it, right? She snorted, and a puff of warm air floated around her face. Guys weren't usually the sharing type. For all she knew, he might be in the same position as she was.

Kate rubbed her bare arms with brisk motions. She definitely needed a longer break from being in Liam's presence, but it was far too cold to hide out here forever.

Something heavy and warm draped over her shoulders.

She jumped, a yelp escaping her lips as she spun around and found Liam.

He gave her a crooked grin. "You need this more than me."

Her gaze dipped to the suit coat, and she pulled it tighter around her shoulders. "Thanks."

Liam brushed some snow from the railing, leaned against it, and stared out at the ice-skating rink below, where the pool would probably have been. They were about three stories up, and the snow was beginning to fall again. He gestured to the rink. "Do you skate?"

Kate wrinkled her nose. "Last time I tried that, I spent more time on my behind than on my feet." She shifted her focus to Liam.

His elbows rested on the edge of the railing, while his hands dangled over the side. He let out a shudder, and his warm breath rose in a cloud around his face.

She reached for the suit coat. "Here, you should take this."

Liam gave her a disgruntled look. "Absolutely not. I'm fine. You need it more than I do."

Kate stilled, holding back a dissent that was on the tip of her tongue. He would probably just get angry if she argued with him—and it was hard not to feel somewhat flattered.

Her gaze ticked from his perfect hair to his sculpted jaw. He wasn't half bad to look at. More than once, she'd thought it was strange he'd come to a couples retreat on his own.

As if he felt her studying him, he looked up and gave her another crooked smile. He straightened, rubbing the back of his neck. "Look, I wanted to say—"

"You don't have to tell me, but—" she blurted.

They both stopped, and she let out a small laugh. "You first."

Liam peered at her, tilting his head slightly. "I wanted to apologize for earlier today. I shouldn't have gone as fast as I did. We could have avoided hitting that ditch."

Her eyes widened for a small moment. "Oh." She adjusted the coat around her. That had been unexpected, and very big of him. She offered a small smile. "I appreciate that."

"Now you."

A lump formed in her throat. She'd lost her nerve to ask him. It might be a really personal issue. Kate cleared her throat and moved her attention to the rink below them once more. "It's nothing really."

"Okay." The tone of his voice implied he still wanted to hear it.

"I shouldn't have even brought it up. Really, it's none of my business—"

The door behind them whooshed open. "Oh, my goodness! Were you two the couple who sang 'Baby, It's Cold Outside'?"

Liam turned slightly and glanced at their intruders. He slipped an arm around Kate's shoulders and pulled her close to him, lighting all kinds of electrical currents from his touch. "That we are," he said with a grin.

The woman was probably in her late forties, and her date looked to be a few years older than her. They were dressed to the nines. She was in a sparkly red-sequined dress with faux fur around the neckline and wrists of her long sleeves. The gentleman wore a suit with a bowtie to match.

Kate bit back a laugh that threatened to bubble from her throat. These two obviously loved Christmas a little too much.

The woman reached over and took Kate's hand in her own. "I simply adore that song and you—" She broke off and brought her fingers to her lips in a chef's kiss. "You were marvelous."

Looking away, Kate felt the blush flood her cheeks. This was another reason she never sang in public.

The woman continued. "Both of you were. You're such a beautiful couple."

"Oh, we're not—"

"Thanks." Liam tightened his hold on her shoulders, and she stiffened. Almost everyone already knew they weren't a couple because of Kate's endless arguments. These two were probably just late to the party.

The gentleman finally piped up. He clapped Liam on the shoulder. "It looks like you're going to get the most points for this event. No one has come close to how well you two did. We wanted to be the first to congratulate you."

Kate's stomach flipped. *Really? They'd gotten the most points so far?* That couldn't be right. They'd failed miserably on the snowmobile ride. Then again, perhaps the points had been awarded for their trip up the mountain and not back. *This might actually work.* She could pull it off with Liam as long as he was serious about helping her.

At some point, the crazy Christmas couple had slipped back inside. Kate whirled around and faced Liam. She opened her mouth, excitement bursting from every part of her.

"I know. I shouldn't have said we were a couple."

Her voice died in her throat. "What?"

"That's what you were going to say, right? You didn't want me to pretend that we're a couple."

Kate frowned. "Oh. Right. Yeah, that was kind of weird." She sliced her hand through the air. "But more importantly, did you hear what they said?" She beamed at him, turning so she could hold both his hands in hers. "They said that our team has the most points. We could *win*."

His lips quirked up. "You're not upset I lied?"

She rolled her eyes and waved him off. "It's not like anyone here *knows* us. And it would probably be more embarrassing to tell them how we ended up being coupled together anyway." She hopped up on the balls of her feet. "If we keep up with this streak, we could win, and I could get the refund

43

for this trip." She couldn't keep the excitement from her voice. "What do you say?"

Liam shrugged. "I wasn't the one who demanded a new partner. What if I said I wasn't on board?"

Her face flushed, and she looked away. That was more than a little mortifying. "I was wrong," she murmured. "I should have—"

"Hey," he murmured as he reached out and grasped her upper arm. "I'm game."

Kate's head popped up, relief washing over her like the first gentle snowfall. A wide smile stretched across her face. "Really? Thanks so much! You won't regret this."

Chapter Ten

Who knew all it would take for Kate to change her mind about him was winning the karaoke event? The light returned to her features, and if possible, she was even more beautiful than she had been on stage.

Liam swallowed hard. *I shouldn't be thinking that way.* Kate wasn't in the right frame of mind to jump into a relationship. But even as she kept babbling excitedly, he knew he was already going down the wrong path. His interest in her had already started, maybe even as early as when they'd sat together on the plane.

Kate sighed. "What other activities are there? I thought I saw ice-skating and cookie decorating. Or was it a gingerbread-house-making contest?"

"Whoa." He placed his hands on her shoulders. "It's all going to work out. Take a breath." This was such a different side of her, and it was absolutely adorable. "But let's rewind a moment. You still haven't told me what you were going to say."

Almost immediately, she seemed to grow uncomfortable. "I don't even know why I thought it was okay to ask—"

"Kate." He laughed. "Just say it."

She took in a deep breath and let it out through pursed lips. Her eyes darted toward the door at the wintery scene around them then back to his face. "I was wondering why you were here alone. I told you my story..." She shook her head. "Of course, if you don't want to tell me, you don't have to. I was just..."

His heart twisted, and his hands dropped to his sides. He'd known it was only a matter of time before she asked. And his wound wasn't as fresh as hers. Liam pushed his hands into his pockets and rocked back on his heels. "It's not a big deal." He raked a hand through his hair. "My girlfriend was really into meteor showers. She found out there would be one this weekend over this area. I booked us this retreat because it was the only way we could guarantee seeing it."

Liam let out a shuddering breath and peeked at her. Saying it out loud was harder than he'd expected. Her eyes were a mask of unreadability. He couldn't tell if she thought it was romantic or if she pitied him. *Why won't she say something? Anything.* The only thing he could read was curiosity. She wanted him to go on.

"Unfortunately, she was diagnosed with stage IV pancreatic cancer and passed away six months ago."

Kate gasped. Her eyes widened, and her hand flew to her mouth. "I'm so sorry," she whispered.

Emotion burned behind his eyes. He hadn't shed tears over Sarah in at least two months. But something about telling Kate his story had dragged all those latent feelings to the surface once again.

The lump in his throat seemed to have grown, and no amount of swallowing could dislodge it. He cleared his throat and spun to face the railing again. Leaning against it, he stared down at the ice-skating rink. "She was a singer too." Peeking at Kate, he offered her a sad smile. "When she sang, I swear angels descended from the clouds to join in."

Kate moved closer and placed her hand on his forearm. She didn't say anything, though it looked like she wished she could. Not surprising. People never knew what to say to someone after hearing this kind of news.

He let out a sad chuckle, pinching the bridge of his nose. "I'm sorry. I completely ruined your excitement. I didn't mean to bring all the doom and gloom on us."

Her hand squeezed where she'd placed it on his arm. "Don't apologize. I'm impressed you came anyway." She bit down on her lower lip. "Do you need the refund too?" Her voice was small, uncertain.

Liam shook his head. "No. I came because I promised her I would." He placed his hand over Kate's. "She insisted that I come no matter what happened to her, so here I am." His voice cracked, and he forced a smile.

Kate blew out another heavy sigh. "That's both terribly romantic and heartbreaking. I don't know if I would have been able to do it. She must have been something special."

"She was." He broke eye contact and glanced down at the skaters again. "It's interesting. Out of everyone I know, you have got to be one of the only ones who seems to understand why this is important. My friends have all told me I need to move on."

"I hear you."

Liam glanced at her again.

She hurried to continue. "My friend says I needed to come for 'closure.'" She muttered something under her breath he didn't quite catch then met his gaze. "Except all I can think about is how this was supposed to be my honeymoon." Her gaze shifted to him then away. "I guess we make quite a pair, huh?"

A crooked smile touched his lips. "I guess we do." She was close enough, he could see the little flecks of amber in her blue eyes. A breeze picked up, tugging on the loose strands of her hair and giving him a whiff of its floral scent.

Without realizing the implications, he reached up and tucked a wayward lock of hair behind her ear. His fingertips brushed against her cool skin, and she shuddered. Liam's gaze dipped down to her lips—the lips she had a habit of nibbling when she seemed nervous about something. Those lips he couldn't help but wonder what it would be like to kiss. Lips he could warm up if given the chance.

"Look, there they are!"

Kate jumped at the interruption. Liam stepped back, forcing himself to put at least two feet between them, then tucked his traitorous hand into his pocket. They both turned as a couple of women scurried up to Kate.

"You were *so* amazing on stage. I was just telling Maddy here that you should sing 'All I Want for Christmas.'"

Mandy's head bobbed enthusiastically. "You would be perfect for that song."

Kate's gaze bounced to Liam, her cheeks filling with a rosy hue.

The first woman reached out and grabbed both Kate's hands in hers. "Come on. No one was as good as you were. It's getting to a point we've contemplated hiding the power cord. We can't stand to listen to one more off-key Christmas song."

Liam's eyes didn't leave Kate's face as she lifted her shoulders in question. He nodded and waved at her to go. She needed this. And if he were honest with himself, he did too.

Chapter Eleven

Kate was still on a high when the night ended. This trip had gone from terrible to absolutely the best night she'd had since breaking up with Theo. Liam had turned out to be a pretty decent guy with a heartbreaking story. She still couldn't fathom what it must have been like to go through what he'd experienced.

Her heart literally ached in her chest for him. She peeked at him again as they made their way back to the elevators from the banquet hall. His hand brushed against hers, sending a shockwave of electricity through her body. Kate yanked her hand closer to her body and clasped it with her other one. Somehow, it felt wrong to experience those kinds of sensations from a guy she barely knew, especially so soon after her own breakup.

Yes, it was definitely wrong to be attracted to him right now. Dang Ansley and her insistence for Kate to move on. Now that was all she could think about. That and her assumption that he might actually kiss her when they were on the balcony. Heat flooded her face, and she turned her head. The last thing she needed was for him to see how much he affected her.

Liam pressed the button on the elevator and shot her a smile. They hadn't spoken since that charged moment. She'd sung a few more songs then called it a night. She needed to talk to Ansley about all these wayward thoughts. Though, if she were honest with herself, she'd admit that her friend would only push her harder.

The elevator doors opened, and they entered, exchanging smiles like the strangers they were. Liam had his hands shoved into his pockets, and he seemed more focused on the shine of his shoes than starting a conversation. That was just as well. The only thing she could think about was whether he was getting closer to dating someone.

Dang it, she needed to stop thinking about that kind of stuff. She was beginning to feel more like a lovesick teenager than the mature woman she was. Based on the way he expressed his frustrations about his friends, it was safe to assume he wasn't dating anyone. But maybe he'd consider dating soon.

Okay, so her thoughts weren't going to behave. There was no controlling them. At least the animosity between them was over. At this rate, only good things could come from her change of perspective. They were getting along now, so potentially, they could win the grand prize.

She shot a look in his direction. "There's an ice-skating activity tomorrow. I've never been ice-skating before, but how hard could it be?"

He murmured and nodded.

"Have you ever been?"

A sheepish grin crossed his face. "I went once when I was ten, and after dislocating my arm, I never went again."

Her eyes widened. "You poor thing."

Liam shrugged. "It's no big deal. I'm sure we'll do just fine."

The elevator doors slid open, revealing their floor. She stepped out, and as they got to the hallway where it split off into left and right, she thumbed toward the former. "This is my way."

"I'll walk you." He said it without a second thought.

She bit back the smile at her lips. *One more point in his favor.* It just went to prove that first impressions weren't all they were cracked up to be. "Thanks," she mumbled.

They arrived at her door, and she stopped, turning to face him. "I'm glad this is working out better. It was a little rough going there, at first."

He flashed her a leg-melting smile. "Me too." Then he stepped forward and tucked a strand of hair behind her ear, much like he'd done when they were outside. Goosebumps rose on her arms, and she let out a shuddered breath. He was inches from her. His deep-green eyes, like two big emerald stones, twinkled. She could get lost in those eyes.

Liam reached forward with both hands. Kate leaned toward him, her eyes fluttering. His hands landed on her shoulders, and he gently removed the jacket he'd let her borrow. Kate's eyes shot open.

"I had a wonderful night, Kate," he whispered. "I'll see you tomorrow for breakfast?"

Fire blazed across her whole face and trailed down her neck. Her whole body was hot with embarrassment. She swallowed the lump in her throat and nodded. "Yes," she wheezed. Clearing her throat, she forced a smile. "Of course. We can put together our game plan—for winning."

He nodded. "Sounds good. I'll meet you down at the breakfast bar around nine."

"Nine." She fumbled for her room key and spun around to save herself any further humiliation.

As soon as the door slammed behind her, she snatched her phone and dialed her friend.

Ansley answered on the second ring. "Kate! I was wondering when you'd call. In fact, I was getting close to calling the hotel myself and ask them—"

"I almost kissed him." Kate paced the hotel room, her now-bare feet slapping against the tile.

"*What?*"

"I don't know what's gotten into me." She placed her palm against her forehead, her voice full of disbelief. "This can't be normal. I must be crazy. I don't do rebounds. But there he was, so sweet and hurting. And we connected on this level..." She groaned and collapsed into a chair in the corner of the room.

"Slow down. What's going on? You kissed *who*?"

Kate groaned again and hurriedly explained the situation at hand. "I can't be having feelings for this guy. I just can't. It's not something I'm capable of. Not only that, but he says he doesn't want to date right now. If he'd wanted to kiss me, he would have. And then there's the fact that he seems to be withholding certain things from me—"

"Maybe you're wrong."

Kate froze. "About what?"

"Give the guy some credit. You barely know each other. You can't expect him to tell you *everything*. Liam told you more than I would have on my first date. Cut him some slack and just go with the flow."

"I can't just go with the flow, Ansley. I plan things. That's what I do." She grew quiet. "I don't want to get hurt again."

Ansley didn't talk for a few minutes, and Kate pulled her phone back to double-check it hadn't died on her again. She'd gotten lucky with this conversation. Finally, her friend spoke up. "The definition of insanity is doing the same thing over and over and expecting a different outcome."

"What does that have to do with anything?"

"Sweetie, I get that you're a planner. But you tried that with Theo. It didn't work. Maybe it's time to try something else." She made a good point.

Kate groaned again. "Maybe you're right."

"Of course, I'm right. Now, what's on the agenda tomorrow?"

She dragged herself from her chair and wandered over to the desk, where the itinerary lay. "Tomorrow morning, there's ice-skating. Then after lunch is a holiday scavenger hunt."

While Ansley prattled on about the last time she'd gone ice-skating, Kate's focus remained on the description of the hunt: be the first to find all thirty items and win a complimentary romantic dinner for two. *Huh. That might actually be kind of fun.*

Chapter Twelve

L iam's heart thrummed in his chest as he sat at the table for breakfast. Familiar guests from the night before floated in and out, grabbing their food and probably heading back to their rooms to eat in peace. He glanced at his watch for the tenth time and blew out an impatient breath. He should have told her to meet him at eight. He hadn't been able to sleep in after last night.

Easy, you're getting too excited. You barely know this woman, and just because you've spent one night spilling your life story doesn't mean she wants anything to do with you.

His legs bounced up and down with nervous energy. Today was ice-skating and the scavenger hunt. But the most exciting part was if they won the hunt, he'd have an excuse to take her to dinner. No matter how hard he tried, he couldn't wipe the smile from his face. He'd held back, as hard as it had been, and hadn't given her a kiss goodnight.

The turmoil and guilt over Sarah had been a driving factor, but also, he didn't know if Kate was interested. Maybe that could change. *Maybe* Tyson had a point and he needed to just get back out there—rip off the proverbial Band-Aid.

Movement out of the corner of his eye caught his attention, and his gaze swiveled to find Kate wandering into the room as if she were floating on clouds. He jolted from his seat and smiled at her.

"Good morning." He dragged his palms down his pants, attempting to dry the clamminess.

"Morning." She eyed him then dropped her focus to the table. "Have you been waiting long?"

"Oh. No, I just got here," he lied. What would she think if she knew he'd been downstairs for a full hour, willing her to make an early appearance just so he could see her face again?

Okay, he was officially losing it. *Time to reel it in.* Liam shook out his hands then wiped them on his pants once more before gesturing toward the kitchen bar. "Shall we?"

She nodded. "I'm starving."

They filled their plates and made it to their table, only to sit across from each other and eat in silence. What had happened? The night before, it had been so easy to talk to her. Now he was a bumbling fool.

He fiddled with his fork, shooting glances in her direction and trying to figure out anything they could talk about.

"My friend—"

"I was thinking—"

They stared at each other and laughed. "You first," she suggested.

Liam examined his fork again. "I was contemplating how nice it was to talk to you last night. I don't think I've opened up to anyone like that since Sarah passed." He lifted his gaze to find her beaming at him, and his whole body warmed. "You have a beautiful smile."

Kate's eyes dipped to her plate, and she tucked some hair behind her ear. "Thanks."

"Now you go."

Her eyes bounced up to meet his then dropped again. "My

friend said some interesting things the other night." She didn't want him to think it was just last night she'd spilled her guts to Ansley about him.

"Yeah?" Liam studied her, his pulse accelerating. She'd talked to her friend, potentially about him. That could be either good or really bad.

Kate blushed. "I can't believe I'm even suggesting this. Please tell me if I'm out of line or if I read the situation wrong. I really don't know what's come over me..."

He reached across the table and rested his hand over hers, successfully putting an end to her rambling. "Just tell me."

She worried her lower lip, her eyes shifting from one thing to another but never quite landing on him. "To paraphrase, she said I should just go with the flow and see where things take me."

Liam's eyes narrowed. "I'm sorry. I don't follow."

Kate let out a strangled laugh. "You're going to think I'm some crazy person. Just forget it."

His hand was still over hers. He wrapped his fingers around hers and gave it a little squeeze. "Hey," he said softly, "you heard all about my crazy stuff. I don't think what you have to say will be any worse than that."

She finally met his eyes, and another chill swept through him. He couldn't dare hope that she might be thinking the same thing he'd been unable to get out of his mind all night.

She took a deep breath and let it out slowly. "I feel like there's this connection between the two of us. I can't explain it, and I've tried to push it away, but it's all I can think about. Maybe it's just this place." She gestured to the resort. "Or maybe it's something more. But either way, I haven't been this at peace in a long time." Her eyes dropped, and her lashes brushed against her cheeks. Kate let out another funny-sounding laugh. "Like I said, I probably sound like a nutjob."

He squeezed her hand again, this time trailing his thumb

over her knuckles until she was forced to look at him once more. "I don't think that sounds crazy at all." He offered her a crooked grin. "It's like *I* said. Last night was refreshing. It was nice to be able to open up to someone and not feel like they were going to judge me or tell me I was doing something wrong."

And just like that, time seemed to slow down. They stared at each other for what seemed like minutes but in actuality were only a few seconds.

"Really?" she asked.

He nodded. "I'd be lying if I said I wasn't excited about seeing you again." He bit back the confession regarding how long he'd waited for her. Clearly, they were both experiencing something neither of them had expected. It would be best not to mess with a good thing. Heck, he was probably at risk for scaring her off as it was.

Her focus shifted to where his hand still held hers. He released her like she'd burned him and placed his hand in his lap. This whole thing was still too new. He needed to ease into that sort of intimacy. Then again, holding himself back from pulling her into his arms and kissing her until she could no longer breathe had been almost impossible. The feelings surging in his body had only continued to grow, however wrong or right they might be.

Of course, he'd take it slow. There was no rushing this sort of thing. They had all week to decide if they wanted to see more of each other when they returned home.

Her soft smile sent another ripple of pleasure though him. Kate put down her fork and picked up her juice. She took a sip, keeping her eye on him over the rim of her cup. "Good. Because I was excited to see you again too."

Chapter Thirteen

Kate's knees buckled, and she lurched forward, a scream building in the back of her throat. Strong arms shot out, and a pair of gloved hands grasped her upper arms. Kate stared into Liam's warm green eyes. The color reminded her of fresh pine needles.

She smiled and looked away. "It seems you are making a habit of saving me from uncertain doom."

Liam chuckled, and the sound was just as inviting as his eyes. They were surrounded by several people in the center of the ice rink. Snow drifted lazily around them, and "Rocking Around the Christmas Tree" played loudly over the speakers.

Why did I think this would be fun? She'd never had the pleasure of ice-skating. She was clumsy enough as it was; she didn't need to add clunky skates and slippery surfaces to the mix. The woven mittens she wore did nothing to disguise Liam's muscles as she rested her hands on his forearms. He was stronger than anyone she'd ever dated.

Dated...

Shaking off the thought and the butterflies that came with it, she forced herself to meet Liam's eyes again. "For someone who hasn't been skating since he was a child, you sure seem sure of yourself."

He skated backward, lifting a shoulder. "Maybe I have good muscle memory."

"Maybe you have good muscles, period," she murmured as she glanced at her feet.

"What?"

Her eyes darted to meet his. *Wait, did I say that out loud?* Heat crept along her cheeks, filling her face, but it didn't matter. It was likely already red from the cold. She released one of his arms and rubbed her nose with the back of her mitten. "Nothing."

Liam gave her a crooked grin as he continued to pull her along with him. "You need to relax. Ease into it. Trust yourself."

"That's easy for you to say. You haven't already fallen down half a dozen times."

"Maybe you just need a quick lesson in skating." Without another word, he pulled her forward then released her. Kate let out a yelp, flinging her arms out at her sides and tracing circles in the air. "Remember," he called, "relax!"

Her eyes widened, and her legs wouldn't cooperate with what her brain was telling them to do. She was headed straight for another skater who had headphones in and wouldn't hear her even if she yelled.

Kate squeezed her eyes shut as tight as she could. Trusting Liam while skating was not one of her brighter moments. Trusting a man at all wasn't wise. She'd learned that over and over. Why would Liam be any different?

Hands tightened around her waist, and she latched on to them with her own. Kate's eyes flew open just as Liam guided her into a turn. He was behind her and a little to the side.

"Don't you *dare* do that again." Her heart hammered in

her chest, beating with the sound of the music. "Promise me you won't let go."

His throaty laugh blew warm breath against her ear and her neck, sending a fresh wave of goosebumps along her skin. His grip tightened on her waist almost protectively. "Promise."

With each turn around the rink, her heartrate slowed to an almost normal pace. Liam's close presence was the only reason for it to skip a few beats here and there. At one point, his hands relaxed, and her own returned to cover them and hold him tightly.

"You don't trust easily, do you?" he asked.

Kate stilled. This conversation wasn't one she'd expected. Though, to be honest, none of this trip had been. But that was the point, according to Ansley—to get the ex out of her system and move on. Marriage was for suckers anyway.

She pressed her lips together, not looking over her shoulder for fear she might give herself away. He knew she was broken. She'd told him herself. Closing her eyes briefly, she let out a slow breath. "No. I don't."

"Does this have something to do with your ex?"

Kate flinched. "What do you think?"

Liam slowed, but his hands never left her waist. Instead, he spun her around to face him, his brows pulled together with concern. "He really did a number on you."

She looked away, that blush creeping back in like a bad infection.

Liam moved one hand to hold hers and the other to grasp her chin, forcing her to look at him. "Hey," he murmured, "you know you can trust me, right?"

She let out a huff. "I barely know you."

"But you can *trust* me." He said it with such conviction, such yearning, she had no choice but to be mesmerized by him. Liam shifted his hand to tuck a strand of hair from her face. "That guy must be one of the dumbest living beings on the planet if he didn't see what he was losing."

She trembled, but because of the cold or because of the way his touch elicited the tremors, she couldn't tell. And frankly, she didn't care.

His gaze dipped to her mouth then bounced back to meet her gaze. A crooked smile touched his lips, and he moved to put a little distance between them. "I'm not going to lie to you. Ever."

"Okay."

Liam tugged her by her hand, moving forward and into the moving sea of skaters. "That being said, I will give you a full disclaimer."

"Okay..." she drawled.

"All guys are dumb. It wasn't just—" He shook his head. "Well, you get the point."

She arched an eyebrow. "*All* guys? Does that include you?"

"Oh. *Most* definitely." He winked at her.

A snicker escaped her lips. Handsome. Funny. Sweet. Liam was the whole package. It wasn't any wonder that he'd already been snatched up by the perfect woman. A woman she would probably never match up to, no matter how hard she tried.

For the moment, she could enjoy what was developing between them. He could see her like no one else ever had. That in and of itself was miraculous. She would be a fool to walk away from it, or worse, get in her own way.

"Hey, look how fast we're going." Liam gestured to her feet.

Against her better judgement, Kate forgot everything she was thinking about, and she looked down. Just like that, she lost her balance. A skate slipped and flew forward as if it had a mind of its own. Or maybe it had a pair of invisible wings.

This created a domino effect, where it felt like the other skate went in a completely different direction.

Viewing her predicament from the outside must have looked quite comedic, but she didn't have time to consider it fully. True to his word, Liam never let go of her hand. The force of her fall was another level entirely, and the two of them slammed down against the ice.

Liam's head bounced against the solid, frozen rink, and she could have sworn she heard a sickening crack.

Just as quickly as she had fallen, she popped back up and flung herself at him. Her hands framed his face. "Liam! Oh my gosh! Are you okay?"

He winced as he peered up at her. His adorable, crooked grin filled his features, and he groaned as he attempted to right himself. "I didn't let go."

"*What*?" She fought the instinct to slug him in the arm. "You should have let go."

His eyes grew serious. "When I make a promise, I don't back out." He lifted his palm and pressed it against his cheek. Another groan escaped his lips, and he winced once more.

Crimson coloring stained her mitten, and she gasped. "Medic! We need a medic over here!" she called, her voice quivering. She brought her gaze down to meet his again. "You're an idiot."

"But a trustful idiot," he interjected with a laugh that turned into a moan. "Maybe I'm just an idiot in love."

Kate sucked in a breath. She couldn't have heard correctly. He hadn't just admitted his feelings for her, right? No. Liam was on the verge of delirium. Or she'd misheard him. Because there was no way he was in love with her. No matter how bad she wanted it to be true.

Chapter Fourteen

Liam lay back on the cot the resort had set up in their only medical office. A man beside him had his teeth clenched tightly as another medic put a splint on his leg. Liam offered him an empathetic smile as he held a compress to a spot on his head just behind his left ear.

He glanced toward the other side of the room, where Kate spoke to the medic who'd seen him just a few minutes prior. His options were two staples or glue. It was going to hurt either way, but honestly, the look on Kate's face hurt more.

His chest felt tight. Yes, he'd had the wind knocked out of him, but that wasn't the reason. The way she kept looking over at him had him on edge. Was she upset he'd spilled how he felt about her? He hadn't thought she'd heard. The confession had escaped his lips before he could lock them up.

It was far too soon to talk about that sort of thing. He'd been in love before, though. He knew what it felt like, and this was it.

If losing Sarah had taught him anything, it was not to waste a single moment living without the person he wanted to be with. His heart pounded, causing his head to beat in the same rhythm. He shut his eyes and lay back against the paper-covered pillow.

Aspirin. All he needed were some painkillers and a little glue, then he'd be right as rain. He just wasn't so sure about Kate. He'd probably royally screwed everything up because he couldn't keep his big mouth shut.

Liam let out a heavy sigh.

A soft hand landed on his forearm, and he jumped. His eyes flew open, and he came face-to-face with Kate. His pulse rushed faster, roaring in his ears, as she leaned over and brushed her warm fingertips across the crown of his head.

"How are you feeling?" she whispered.

He reached up with his free hand and grasped hers, bringing her fingertips down to his lips. Pressing a kiss to them, he murmured, "Better now." His gaze remained locked on hers, gauging her reaction to his actions. There was no denying a response, however small. Her cheeks colored, and she looked away. But she allowed him to continue holding her hand.

"Kate, I wanted—"

"Mr. Harper, how are you feeling?"

Kate's head snapped up at the intrusion, then she stepped back. Liam's grip remained firm, not allowing her to escape. He slowly dragged his attention to the man who'd so rudely intruded.

The nametag he wore said Dr. Wong. The smile lines were deep around his eyes as he reached for the compress Liam held. "It looks better already. We'll close this up, and you'll be free to go. We don't want to keep you from the festivities." He winked at Kate.

"Actually, you should probably get some rest. You're probably in a great deal of pain, and -"

Liam squeezed her hand. "I'm fine."

Her brows pinched. "You cut your head open. You were bleeding all over the rink."

"Kate," he admonished. "It's a scratch. It'll heal. I'm not going to miss out on another second I can spend with you."

Her mouth opened, closed, then opened again, but nothing came out.

Dr. Wong looked between the two of them. "Your wife is right. You should probably take it easy today."

Both of their eyes swiveled toward him.

"Oh, we're not—" they started in unison, but the argument seemed to die just as it had started.

They exchanged smiles before Liam glanced back at the doctor. "Is there a medical reason why I can't continue as usual with my day? Will I be at risk of passing out? Do I have a concussion? Or something that risks my health further?"

"Well, *no*."

Liam flashed the doctor a smile. "Wonderful. Then that settles it. Give me some painkillers and some glue, and we'll be on our way."

"Liam—" Kate's voice held a note of exasperation.

Once more, he brought her hand to his lips. "Relax, darling. I've been through worse." As if in direct argument to his statement, he winced.

Kate gave him an exasperated look and shook her head. "Fine. But the scavenger hunt isn't for a few more hours. You're going straight back to the hotel room and resting until it starts."

"Deal." Liam met the doctor's eyes once more. "You heard the woman. Fix me up so I can get out of here."

Dr. Wong nodded. "This is going to sting just a little bit..."

Liam didn't hear another word the man said. In fact, he barely felt anything. His eyes remained glued to Kate's, and all he could think about was what might be going through her head. Her features were a mask of unreadability. He couldn't tell what she was thinking, no matter how hard he tried.

The fact that she was by his side demanding that he take care of himself was a good sign, though. It was something he could build on. Baby steps. Liam pulled her hand from his lips and flattened her palm against his cheek. His hand covered hers, holding her there so she was forced to move in closer.

She offered him another small smile and looked away as she settled on the edge of his cot. This whole situation wasn't bad at all. There were definitely worse things than being looked after by a beautiful, smart woman.

Kate walked him into his hotel room. As she led him toward the bedroom, he resisted. When she gave him a funny look, he gestured toward the sitting room with the couch. "I'd rather stay out here. I don't want to get so comfortable, I can't make it to the scavenger hunt."

She shook her head. "Oh no, you don't. Your health is more important than some scavenger hunt."

He set his stony gaze on hers once more. "I made a promise, Kate. I don't back out, remember?"

"Vividly." She sighed and looked around the room. "I'm not letting you rest on the couch. But what if I stay here while you take a nap? I'll wake you when it's time to go."

"Promise?" He took both her hands in his. "You need to promise me, or I won't agree to it." He bit back a smile.

Kate rolled her eyes and let out an exaggerated groan. "I *pinky swear* I will get you when it's time to head down for the scavenger hunt. Now, go take a nap before I admit I had my fingers crossed."

He shot her a steely stare.

She let out a laugh that warmed him right to his core. "Just *go*."

Chapter Fifteen

"All right, folks. This is the event you've been waiting for. Not only will you get points for the grand prize, but the lucky couple to win this scavenger hunt will get an all-expenses-paid date night." The woman held up a stack of five-by-seven cards. "I have in my hand the list of items you will need to find in order to win. The first couple who returns with photos of everything on this card will be the winners. If no one finds every item, then the team with the most will win. In the case of a tie, the resort has agreed to give both winning teams the prize."

Applause filled the lobby of the resort. Kate glanced around the room. It seemed to be full of more couples than she'd remembered. That meant more people to compete against. Kate took in a deep breath and let it out slowly, attempting to calm her nerves.

Liam squeezed her hand, drawing her attention. He grinned at her, winked, then brought her hand to his lips.

Just like that, all her worries and anxiety slipped away. She didn't have to win this event. In fact, if she didn't win the grand prize, that would be okay too. Truth be told, she had stayed in hopes of getting her money back, but if she hadn't come, then she would never have met Liam.

Kate squeezed his hand back and returned his smile with one of her own. She'd found something she'd never thought possible.

The woman with the cards passed them out facedown. "On my mark, you may flip your cards over and begin." She scanned the room, her eyes meeting each team before her face broke into a wide smile, and she lifted a whistle to her lips.

Everyone around them flipped over their cards and took off. Liam turned over their card, but Kate placed her hand over the top. "We don't have to do it if you don't want to."

His brows creased together, then a grin stretched across his face. "The heck we don't. We're winning this if it's the last thing we do."

She let out a laugh and removed her hand.

Liam held up the card. "The first is a golden heart. I saw some decorations down the hall from that banquet hall where we'd had dinner the first night. Let's go." He grabbed her hand and dragged her toward the elevator. Liam pushed the button, but Kate shook her head.

"Let's take the stairs."

They darted around the corner of the elevator and headed into the stairwell. Her laughter echoed up the shaft as they breathlessly took the stairs two at a time.

The heart decorations were just where Liam had seen them. The next several items were miscellaneous objects they'd seen or used since their arrival: the snowmobiles, a dinner setting, a pair of ice skates, and a picture of themselves in front of the resort sign.

She lost track of time with each item they checked off the list. Liam was goofy and fun, and he could make her forget everything that had been weighing down on her. It was funny how one person could so easily change the way she felt about the world.

"We've got one left."

"What is it?" Kate leaned closer to get a look at the list.

Liam's brows knit together. He tilted the card for her to look at. "It says a Christmas kiss."

She let out a laugh. "A *Christmas* kiss? What does that even mean? It's not Christmas yet."

He scratched his head. "I'm not sure."

"Well, it's our last item. If we figure it out, we might have a chance at winning." She danced from side to side, shaking out her hands. "So, let's figure it out."

They were outside near the ice rink. She barely felt the cold air as it swirled around the two of them. Snow had begun to fall, and the night sky was darkening.

His eyes brightened. "I got it. Come on!" He took her hand, lacing his fingers within hers. They hurried toward the front doors of the resort.

"What is it?" She called.

"You'll see." He tugged her through the lobby and stopped beside the Christmas tree that rose fifteen feet high beside the fireplace. His green eyes were the same color as the pine.

She glanced at the tree then at Liam. "A kiss in front of the tree? Do you really think that's what they mean?"

He shook his head. Liam pulled her backward so they stood directly in front of the fireplace. Without saying a word, he pointed his finger up.

Kate lifted her face and peered at a small sprig of green leaves. Her eyes widened, and she brought her gaze to meet his. "Mistletoe!" she breathed. "Liam, you're a genius." She glanced back at the leaves, then the smile dropped from her face at the implication of what was about to happen. A Christmas kiss. It was obvious the organizers were expecting

69

each of the couples to participate in this. It was probably part of some big publicity stunt.

She gave him a shy smile, her gaze dropping to the ground. "You don't have to do—"

Without warning, Liam placed his hands on either side of her face and pulled her close. He pressed his lips to hers, warm and full of desire. Kissing Liam was like nothing she'd ever experienced in her entire life. He was gentle and sweet, but full of fire at the same time. He could make her laugh one second and make her want to throw something at him in the next. He was everything she never knew she needed.

Her heart thundered, and her skin tingled where he held her. How had she gotten so lucky to snag a guy as good as Liam? There was this way he had about himself. Deep down, she knew she could trust him with her heart and her whole being. It was like his touch and that smile could make the world as she knew it stop spinning. Kate wrapped her arms around his neck and threaded her fingers through his hair. She could get lost in this moment if she let herself, and she would have if he hadn't been the one to stop.

Liam's kiss shifted from fervent to sweet. He loosened his hold on her and pulled back, pressing his forehead against hers. His husky voice sent chills down her spine. "Don't you *ever* tell me I don't have to kiss you like that."

Kate took in a shaky breath. "Okay."

He cupped her face with his hand and grazed her cheekbone with his thumb. The corners of his lips twitched, lifting into a humorous smile. "We forgot to get a picture." He pulled out his phone and tapped the screen to flip the camera for a selfie. Meeting her eyes, studying her as if to ask for permission, he paused. "Are you ready?"

Kate nodded, pressing her lips into a firm line.

He hooked his finger under her chin and lifted it, sending

all kinds of electrical pulses through her body. She let her eyes flutter closed as he brushed his lips against hers.

Chapter Sixteen

L iam couldn't stop staring at her. She was so beautiful, and he couldn't believe he hadn't seen it at the airport. He'd been so blinded by his own pain over Sarah that he hadn't been willing to consider there was someone else out there.

What were the odds that he could fall in love with two amazing women in one lifetime? He didn't know, but he didn't think he'd luck out a third time.

They sat across from each other at a small table for two. Beside them was a large window that showed off the ice-skating rink covered in lights. If the sun were still up, they'd probably have a view of the mountain range—not that he'd be looking at it.

Kate's lips quirked into a soft smile as she lifted her glass of water to her lips. "I can't believe we were the only ones who took a mistletoe picture."

He lifted a shoulder. "I guess we're just lucky."

She swallowed and shook her head. "No. You're *smart*. I would have never thought of it." Her eyes lowered, and her lashes rested against her now-rosy cheeks. "Can I ask you something?"

Liam chuckled. He reached across the table and grasped her hand in his. Letting his thumb trail over her knuckles, he nodded. "Of course."

Kate bit down on her lower lip. "Never mind. It's silly." She tugged on her hand, attempting to release it from his grasp, but he kept it securely within his own.

"Just ask me."

She lifted her gaze to meet his. "What is this, exactly?"

"*This?*" His features pinched.

Her blush deepened, and she looked away. "I sound like a total idiot."

"Don't say that. What are you referring to?"

Kate sighed. "*This.* Whatever has developed between us over the last two days. Is it some infatuation? Something a little deeper?" Her voice dropped so that he could barely hear it. "A fling?"

His brows shot up. "What? Of course not." He scooted in his chair and leaned closer to her. "I like you, Kate. I *really* like you." The pounding in his chest couldn't be good for his heart. He hadn't dated anyone since Sarah, but he felt like he could finally be ready to. It had just taken finding the right girl to get him there.

Her gaze cut to his, but she didn't respond. That didn't seem very good. What was she thinking? He couldn't tell if she liked the idea or if she wanted to hightail it out of there and never see him again. The not knowing was wreaking havoc with everything bouncing around in his body.

Liam finally released her hand and ran his own hand through his hair. He didn't know what he would do if she disagreed with him. After their kiss, there was only one thing he wanted. More. Not just more kisses, but more of her. More laughter. More fun. More of Kate.

He looked away then returned his attention to her. "*This* —whatever it may be—is something I want to explore further. I don't want us to go home and pretend none of this happened. I want to see where *this* can go."

"I'd like that too."

Her whispered admission caused a flood of relief to wash over him. It was hot and cold all at once, and he reveled in it. "You do?" he asked, leaning forward again. "Really? Because you don't have to if—"

She reached across the table and placed her palm against his cheek. "Don't tell me I don't have to want this, whatever it is." Her face scrunched into an adorable grimace. "That sounded so much better in my head."

He turned his face into her hand and kissed her palm. "It sounded perfect to me."

Their waiter arrived with their food, and their conversation died down as they began their meal. The silence wasn't something he felt he needed to fill. It had been a long time since he'd been able to spend time with someone and be content to *just be*.

Her eyes met his several times across the table, and each time filled him with a thrilling spark, a yearning for something more. His phone buzzed on the table, lighting up. They both glanced at it for a moment, but he let it be. Whoever it was, they weren't as important as the time he was spending with her. He'd respond to it later.

A few minutes passed, and it buzzed again. Kate pointed to his phone with her fork. "You can get that if you want. I'm not some crazy person who needs your attention all the time."

Liam snickered. "I wouldn't mind if you were, but no. I don't need to get it. I'm here with you."

The smile she gave him, the way her eyes brightened, confirmed he'd made the right choice. She was more important than anything or anyone who might be trying to contact him. It was probably just Tyson.

Tyson. Shoot. It probably *was* Tyson reminding him about the date he'd set up with Rebecca. He'd have to shut that down the second he got back to his room. Thank goodness they hadn't gone on a date or interacted much on the phone. There would be less conflict in ending something that hadn't even started.

When he glanced back at Kate, she was giving him a strange look. Her eyes were more squinted as she studied him, and her head was tilted slightly to the side. She held the prongs of the fork between her lips, and it was almost like she didn't realize what she was doing.

Liam waved his hand in front of her face. "You okay?"

She jumped, her eyes more focused. "Yep."

"Tomorrow, we have a few more events to win if you want that grand prize."

Kate lifted a shoulder and stabbed at her salad. "You know, I don't really care about that so much." Her eyes darted to meet his then dropped. "I just want to spend as much time as I can with you."

He put down his fork and brought his glass to his lips. He took a small sip. "I can't argue with that. But what would you say if I told you that you could have both?"

As expected, her face brightened. "You're too good for me." Then she grew serious and looked around the room. "But seriously, where are the hidden cameras?"

"What?" he laughed.

"You know. The cameras catching all of this. You're a plant, right? I'm being pranked."

Liam leaned across the table again, the humor gone from his voice. "I can assure you there is no such thing. I'm as real as they come."

She cocked her head to the side. "Then maybe you're right."

"Right about what?"

"Luck. You said I'm the lucky one."

He wagged his finger at her. "*No*, I said *we're* lucky."

She lifted her glass toward him. "Okay. *We're* lucky." Truer words had never been spoken. He'd never argue that luck didn't exist ever again. She motioned to his phone. "I have a strange favor to ask."

"Oh?"

Her cheeks pinked. "I left my purse in the hotel room. Can I send my friend one of the pictures you took? The one in front of the tree outside? She's a sucker for that sort of stuff."

He unlocked his phone and pushed it across the table. "Of course."

Kate grinned and retrieved the phone. She swiped through the pictures until she found the perfect one. She typed out a short message then handed the phone back. "Thank you."

Liam grabbed his napkin from his lap and dabbed his mouth. He rose from his chair. "I'm going to run to the bathroom." Her eyes followed him as he pushed in his chair and walked around the table. He dipped down and pressed a kiss to the crown of her head. "I'll be right back."

"You better be."

Chapter Seventeen

Kate picked up her glass, watching Liam walk away and marveling at how quickly her upside-down life had turned right-side up. Who knew that when Ansley had told her to get her ex out of her system that Kate would find someone new—someone better?

Liam's phone vibrated, lighting up on the far side of the table. Kate's eyes drifted toward it. Whoever it was had been persistent. She loved that Liam wasn't the kind of guy who was glued to his phone. It had been sweet of him to decline the calls or messages he was getting while they were on their date.

However, when someone was as insistent as this person was, then it had to be important. She looked over her shoulder where Liam had left. When he got back, she'd tell him to just go ahead and get back to his friend.

She waited for another minute or two when a woman seated in a table nearby leaned over. "I'm so sorry, but do you have the time?"

Reflexively, Kate reached for her purse then remembered she'd left it in her hotel room. Without thinking, she reached over the table and picked up Liam's phone. "Six forty-three."

The woman smiled with appreciation and resituated herself in her seat. At that very moment, another message popped up on the screen.

Rebecca: *I can't wait for our date when you get back in town.*

Kate nearly dropped the phone as her fingers grew weak. Her heart hammered, and she fumbled with the phone to return it to its place near Liam's seat. Her hands trembled under the table, and she swallowed hard. Who was Rebecca? Rebecca who had added several heart emojis to her message. Rebecca who was probably tall and thin and prettier than Kate.

Kate's blood ran cold. There had to be a reasonable explanation. Or this could be exactly what it looked like. Liam was seeing someone. It might not be serious. For all she knew, he was seeing several women. She sucked in a shuddering breath, her thoughts immediately drifting to when she'd found out that there was another woman in her fiancé's life.

This couldn't be happening. Not again. Not to her. She fidgeted in her seat, her eyes darting toward the exit of the restaurant and back to the food on the table. She'd been a complete fool to think this was more than it was. Liam hadn't defined what this relationship was, and neither had she.

Relationship. Ha. That's rich. This isn't a relationship. This is one of those flings people have on vacation when they know they won't have to see the person again.

Her face burned with the acknowledgement that this was exactly that. Footsteps approached, along with the burning sensation right behind her eyes. What a darn fool she'd been.

Liam pulled out his chair and lowered himself into it. He flashed her that smile. The smile that was so good at making her legs go weak. That smile that made her want to give him the world.

And her heart shattered.

His brow creased. "Is everything okay?"

"Hmm? What?" She cleared her throat of all the emotion that had built up. "Of course. I'm fine." She forced a smile, but it only made the tightness in her chest worse. She lifted her glass to her lips and took another small sip.

Escape—that was what she needed to do. She had to get out of there before she crumpled into a heap on the floor. Her heart hadn't been strong enough to fall for another guy so soon, and now she hated herself for it.

Worse, Ansley would tell her, "I told you so" before the night was up if she'd known how dangerously fast this had all progressed.

Kate swallowed hard against the lump in her throat and placed two fingers at her temple.

Liam leaned forward. "Are you sure you're okay? You look sick." He reached for her hand, and she jerked it away from him. His features tightened; a flicker of pain or something deeper flashed behind his eyes.

Good. He should be upset. Knowing she'd caused it only made her stomach churn harder, though. She nodded and pushed out her chair. "Maybe you're right. I need some fresh air."

He rose from his seat. "I'll come with you."

"No!"

His head reared back. "Kate?"

She held up a hand to interrupt him, then closed it to hold up a single finger. "I'll only be a few minutes." Her eyes pleaded with him. "Just a few minutes."

Liam's jaw tightened. He didn't return to his seat. Nor did he move a muscle.

"Please," she murmured.

Slowly, he dropped back into his chair and nodded. "If you're not back in five minutes, I'm coming to look for you."

That was fine, because in five minutes, she'd probably be

in her room, hiding from him. This whole situation was mortifying. She couldn't believe she'd allowed herself to fall so hard for a stranger. A stranger! Because that was really all he was. Yes, she knew about his past with the woman he'd loved. She'd grown closer to him with each thing he shared about himself.

But how much could she really trust him? For all she knew, he had been lying the whole time. He'd never mentioned a Rebecca. He'd never mentioned that he had a girl back home.

She scurried from the restaurant, ignoring the double doors that would have led her out onto the balcony to the fresh air she so desperately needed. Instead, she kicked off her heels and sprinted toward the elevator.

Her heart pounded with each step she took. There were still a few days left for this retreat. They were in the lead for that grand prize, and if she left now, she'd forfeit everything. Right now, the important thing would be to figure out how to keep her distance from Liam even though she'd have to spend two more days with him. She'd have to teach herself not to get goosebumps when he brushed against her. She'd have to force herself not to lean toward him when he was close enough to kiss her.

She'd have to construct a wall and fast, because if she didn't, her heart wouldn't only be shattered. It would be utterly destroyed. And she'd have to do all of this without him knowing. If he found out that she'd fallen for him, he'd probably just laugh at her.

Kate made it up to her hotel room and hurried inside. She stripped out of her dress and made a beeline for the shower. She stood beneath the showerhead, letting the tears mix with the drizzling hot water that poured over her in the dark. Legs giving out beneath her, she sunk to the floor. Her knees were brought up to her chest, and she buried her face into them. For now, she'd allow herself to be vulnerable—away from prying, beautiful green eyes. Then tomorrow, she'd pretend like nothing had happened.

Chapter Eighteen

L iam glanced at his phone again. Kate had been gone for seven minutes. He'd said five, but he knew something had happened, and she wasn't ready to share with him. If he'd learned anything while dating Sarah, it was that when a girl needed a moment to compose herself, he needed to let her have it.

He tapped his feet impatiently. How long should he let her have? This relationship was far too new for him to know what Kate would need. What if she needed him to hold her, to wrap his arms around her and tell her that everything would be all right? Had she gotten a call while he was in the restroom? Someone in her family could be hurt.

Liam jolted from his seat and threw down his napkin. That was it. He couldn't just sit back and let her deal with something so obviously hurting her all alone. She needed him. He moved through the restaurant toward the double doors that led to the balcony. When he reached the outside, he looked both ways down each side, but it was completely empty.

Confusion swirled within him. He stepped back inside and hailed a waiter. "Did you see a woman come out here a few minutes ago?"

The waiter shook his head. "I'm sorry, sir. No one has been out on the balcony this evening."

A heavy weight settled into the pit of his stomach. Kate was dealing with something, and it had to be bad if she'd left without so much as a word. He darted back to his table, left a tip, and grabbed his jacket. Then he headed for the exit. Wherever Kate was, she was alone, and she needed him. He could feel it right down to his toes.

Liam couldn't get to the elevator fast enough. She had to be headed to her hotel room. That was the only place that would give her the privacy she'd need to work through whatever was bothering her. He forced himself to walk, though doing so was almost as painful as watching Kate struggle at dinner. The hotel management wouldn't take too kindly to him running through the lobby like he had to put out a fire, but with each passing minute, he wasted precious time.

The dark feeling shifted and contorted until it was no longer just in his stomach. It had settled over his shoulders and clouded his vision. Worst case scenario: someone could be dying. He'd been through that before, and he could help her.

His footsteps slowed. What if her ex wanted her back? He attempted to shake off that notion, but like a vulture, it circled overhead. That worm could have called her and told her he was sorry and wanted to come meet her. Or he wanted her to come home—to him.

Liam's hands balled into fists. That man wasn't good enough for Kate. He'd proven it already. And by her reaction, she wasn't thrilled about what had happened.

Several more depressing thoughts raced through his head, each one weighing him down even more. The only way to set this right would be to talk to her. He was making himself sick with every new idea that passed through him.

He made it up to her hotel room and took a deep breath. He couldn't be on edge, not if she was working through it. Adding to her pain was the last thing he needed to do right now. He lifted his fist and knocked on the solid wooden door.

There was no noise from within the hotel room. Out in the hallway, no one wandered to their rooms. It was too quiet, setting him even more on edge. He swallowed around the lump forming in his throat and knocked harder this time. "Kate, I know you're in there."

Still nothing. He glanced down the hall both ways. Maybe he was wrong. Kate could have gone to the bathroom instead of the balcony. But she hadn't gone in the direction of the bathroom. What if he'd missed her? He could go back down there and wait.

Instinct told him Kate was in her room. He could feel it just like he'd been able to feel that Sarah was ending her chemo even when she hadn't told him yet.

His jaw tightened, and he worked it back and forth. He could go down to the lobby and ask for a key to her room. Heck, he could call the front desk right now and tell them he thought she might need help.

But that wasn't his style. Fighting the urge to pound on her door and yell for her to open it, he turned and leaned against it. Folding his arms, he focused on calming the anxiety that had wrapped around his throat like a noose.

"I'm not going anywhere, Kate," he muttered. "Take as long as you want. When you're ready to come out and talk, I'll be—"

The door handle clicked. He jumped away from his position and spun around as she pulled open the door. Kate's hair was wet, hanging around her face. Her cheeks and the area around her eyes were blotchy, but because of a hot shower or because of tears, he couldn't tell.

She peered at him through the open doorway, not letting him in or coming out to speak to him.

He frowned, searching her eyes for any hint at what she was going through. "Are you okay?"

Kate shrugged, giving him a short nod. "Of course. Why wouldn't I be?"

"You left. You just—" He raked a hand through his hair. "I've been around the block before, Kate. Something's bothering you, and it's not some small thing." He blew out a harsh breath. "I can't help you if you won't talk to me."

Her eyes hardened. "Don't pretend you know me, Liam. When I say I'm fine, accept it."

His head reared back. The tone of her voice held a bite to it that stung more than he wanted to admit. He took a step closer to her room. Her eyes widened briefly, like she was scared he would force himself inside, but then her expression cooled, leaving no trace of that fear.

Liam reached out and brushed his thumb down her jaw. "I care about you. That means I can worry about you too."

She pulled her head back. "Well, you don't have to." She sighed, and her gaze softened somewhat. "I'm tired. It's been a long day, and I just want to go to bed." Her voice cracked, and she sucked in a breath before blowing it through pursed lips. A smile filled her face, but it didn't meet her eyes. Fake. All of it was fake. "I'll see you tomorrow for the cookie-decorating contest, okay?"

His jaw clenched. Something deep inside him told him leaving her like this was a bad idea. A very bad idea. If he didn't clear the air now, things would only get worse. But what could he do? It wasn't like he could force her to tell him what was going on. If she didn't want to trust him, he couldn't make her, no matter how much he wanted to.

They stood for what felt like several minutes. Then she broke eye contact and stared at the floor. "Fine." He spun on his heel and took a few steps down the hall.

"Thank you for dinner, Liam," she whispered.

He froze, not looking back. He knew if he did, he wouldn't be able to leave again.

Chapter Nineteen

K ate paced her hotel room. She couldn't go down there. Not now. Not after last night. Why on earth had she agreed to seeing him? She should just go home early. But then Ansley would probably tear her a new one for not seeing this through.

Her hands balled into fists, and her pace quickened. This wasn't up to Ansley. She didn't know what Kate was going through. If their situations were flipped, Ansley would probably already be halfway home to Maine by now.

She stopped in her tracks and stared at her phone on the edge of the side table. Chances were slim she'd be able to have a full conversation with Ansley if she tried calling. But at this point, she didn't care if she had to dial her friend's number a dozen times to get the point across.

Kate strode across the room and snatched the phone off the table. Ansley answered on the first ring.

"Finally! Are you going to tell me more about whose number you used to send that photo? Please tell me it was that guy you almost kissed. You kissed him, right?"

"I'm coming home."

"Wait. What?" Ansley let out a laugh. "Does this have something to do with the guy?"

Kate collapsed onto the edge of her bed. "Of course it has something to do with the guy." Her voice rose in pitch. "I can't stay here anymore. I wasn't ready, and we both knew it."

"Whoa, slow down, Kate. What happened?"

"I fell for him, *okay*? Hard and fast, and it shouldn't have even happened." She'd been an idiot. The first rule of getting over an ex was not falling for someone new. And yet, here she was with a scar on her heart that hadn't healed yet before she'd slashed a fresh one.

Ansley let out a soft chuckle, pulling her from her spiraling thoughts. "Well, we sort of knew it *could* happen, right? You *had* almost kissed him."

"I *did* kiss him." Kate grimaced. This was so much worse now that she was telling Ansley.

Her friend let out a slow whistle. "How was it?"

"*Ansley!*"

"What?" Her voice was genuinely curious, but the intrigue practically dripped from her one-word question.

"He's *dating* someone. Someone *else*. That's what."

For the first time during this conversation, Ansley didn't seem to have a snarky comeback. "Are you sure? I mean, it could have been a friend or a family member."

"Of course I'm sure. I saw a message from her on his phone. Some woman named Rebecca." She let out a sharp laugh. "What do you think 'I can't wait for our date' means?" Pain sliced through her chest, making it hard to breathe. Saying the woman's name left a sour taste in her mouth. "He's just like Theo." Her voice broke.

"Kate, sweetie, I'm sure he's not—"

"Why do I keep falling for the wrong guys?" She pinched the bridge of her nose and squeezed her eyes shut. "I need you to help me get a flight out of here today. I don't even care that I won't get my money back. It's not worth it anymore." Kate jumped from her place on the bed and paced the room again. "I thought he was different. I mean, I *really* thought there could be something between us, Ansley. I feel so *stupid*. That's why I need to come home. I can't see him again. I just... *can't*." The last word came out in a painful whisper.

"Are you sure? What if you tried avoiding him? You could find someone else to hang with and make sure you're not alone with him. Or..." It seemed even Ansley had figured out Kate's options were limited.

Kate shook her head. "I *have* to leave. If I'm forced to see him again, I don't think my heart would be able to take it. I might do something really stupid."

"Like what?"

Letting out a heavy sigh, Kate slowed her steps. "I could allow myself to fall back into bad habits. I might rationalize that he's choosing me over this other girl. But we both know that rarely works out for anyone."

"Okay," Ansley murmured.

"Okay, what?" Kate rubbed the back of her neck.

"I'll call the airline and see what I can do."

Kate straightened, hope blooming in her chest. "Really?"

"*Of course*. I love you, Katy Girl. When I get the itinerary, I'll email it to you."

Biting back the emotion in her throat, Kate allowed a tear to slip down her cheek. "Love you too, Ansley."

"Chin up, sweetie. Things will get better."

Kate nodded. "I know..." Her voice broke. "I'll see you soon."

She hung up the phone and glanced around her hotel room. It wouldn't take much to pack up. The only thing holding her up was her prospective schedule. The flight could leave in a few hours or later that evening. Heck, it could leave first thing in the morning, and she didn't want to pack everything up only to have to go digging for something she needed.

Carefully, she settled back onto the edge of her bed, then she lay down and stared at the ceiling. Salty tears slid from the corners of her eyes and into her hairline. This was the right decision. The financial loss would hurt, but not as much as the pain caused by yet another dishonest man.

In a few years, maybe she would open her heart and try again.

Chapter Twenty

T he clock on the wall of the ballroom read ten after ten in the morning. Kate was supposed to be here by now. Liam figured she might be a little later this morning based on how she'd reacted last night when he'd confronted her after dinner. But at this point, he wasn't sure if he should go looking for her or give her another couple minutes.

The organizer for the event stopped by his table and flashed him a smile. She tucked a strand of hair behind her ear, and her gaze trailed over the room. "Is your partner here yet?"

Liam cleared his throat and shook his head. "She was feeling under the weather last night."

She frowned, tilting her head to the side. "I'm sorry to hear that." Her gaze dipped to the tray of cookies and the brightly colored frosting. "If she doesn't show up in the next ten minutes, your team will forfeit. Do you think she's on her way?"

Liam's attention shifted to the clock on the wall again. "Would you be able to hold off long enough for me to go get her? Maybe she slept through her alarm."

The woman clicked her tongue and shook her head. "Unfortunately, we have to start right on time. But if you think you can track her down and get back on time, you're welcome to try."

He shifted his weight from one foot to the other, almost dancing as he fidgeted. This was something Kate had wanted. He wasn't as invested in winning as she had been. If she didn't want to show for this event, she was practically demonstrating that she'd lost interest.

The only thing that didn't sit right with him was the fact that she hadn't called. *Wait. Does she even have my number?* That didn't matter. Kate was the kind of woman who would have come down to tell him she wasn't interested anymore. She wouldn't leave him hanging... would she?

That thought made his stomach churn. He hadn't thought she would abandon him. The feeling was similar to when Sarah had left him. Granted, she'd left him under different circumstances. She hadn't had a choice. It was strange to feel an almost identical sting.

His jaw tightened, and he gave the woman a sharp nod. "I'll see what I can do." Without waiting for a response, he headed straight for the double doors. The cacophony of excited voices died away as he neared the elevator. One of the things he'd liked about Kate was how thoughtful she was. He loved that he could talk to her.

But last night, she'd shown a completely different, unexpected side to her. She'd thrown up some walls and refused to talk to him. Something was going on. He didn't know what it was, but now he was going to find out. She didn't have the luxury of keeping this secret. Not anymore.

He didn't care if they barely knew one another. She would talk to him and bring everything out into the open.

The elevator doors opened, and he half-expected to find her standing there with a chagrined smile on her face. His heart dropped when the elevator stood empty before him. She wasn't coming.

His disappointment quickly shifted into something foreign and distasteful. Fury swirled in his gut, mixing with the disappointment and something else. Pain.

Okay, he was jumping to conclusions. What if she really was sick? For all he knew, she could be hovering over a toilet, her skin pale. As much as he didn't want her to be suffering, that idea sat better with him. That would be a better excuse for standing him up.

Liam made it to her room and knocked on the door. He glanced down the hallway, not finding any activity. He hadn't passed her on the way down. There was a chance she'd gone somewhere else to be alone.

He shook off that thought. *She would have told me,* he insisted to himself. His attempt to swallow the lump in the back of his throat was a sad one. It continued to grow, and he almost felt like the air around him was being sucked into a vortex.

This time, he clenched his hand into a fist and thudded it on the door, making sure to keep his voice controlled. "Kate!" he called. "Kate, I need to speak to you." The last thing he needed was to scare her off.

Something crashed in her room, and his heart jumped into his throat. She was in there. Relief and concern were quickly replaced by that familiar aching in his chest. "Kate!" He pounded on the door again. "I'm not leaving until you talk to me."

The door swooshed open, and she stood before him with red-rimmed eyes. Black mascara smudged beneath her eyes and her brows lowered. "What do you think you're doing?" she hissed as she poked her head into the hall and looked both ways. "You're going to get us in trouble."

His features softened as he took a step forward and pushed on her door. "We need to talk."

Kate gasped and jumped out of the way. She hovered near the door, her back pressed against the wall.

Liam turned around and faced her, his arms crossed tightly against his chest if only to prevent him from pulling her into his arms and asking what he could do to fix whatever had happened. She'd been crying, and by the looks of it, she hadn't gotten much sleep either.

Her dark eyes flitted around the room then came to land on him briefly before falling to the floor. "What do you want, Liam?"

He let out a sound that resembled a disbelieving laugh blended with a huff. "What?"

She forced a heavy sigh. "You're the one who wants to talk. What is it?"

Liam stared at her dumbfounded. "I don't know."

Kate's features scrunched up. "You came to talk, and you don't know what you want to talk about?"

He jabbed a finger at the door. "You said you were going to be at the cookie decorating thing, and you stood me up."

The angry, defensive expression fell from her face, and she looked at the floor again.

"Yeah. Let's start there." He lifted his chin. "Why didn't you show?"

"Maybe I didn't want to waste my time anymore."

Liam shook his head. "What is that supposed to mean?"

She lifted a shoulder. "I'm not going to win anyway. What's the point?"

His brows creased, and he took a step toward her. She stiffened, causing him to stop before he got too close. "What's the matter, Kate? Why won't you talk to me?" He couldn't hide the pain in his voice. It was like his chest had been torn open. He was allowing her to see exactly how he felt. And surprisingly, he didn't care, not if it would help. "Kate... please tell me what happened," he whispered.

Her head jerked up and she shot an angry look at him. "You want to know what happened? Men. That's what happened." Her voice was loud and full of rage.

His hands dropped to his sides, helpless. What was he supposed to say to that?

She took a step toward him, closing the distance between them, and poked him hard in the chest. "There are no good men left in this world, and you proved it last night."

"*What*?" He grabbed her wrist with his hand.

Kate attempted to turn away from him, but he pulled on her, forcing her to take another small step toward him.

"What on earth are you talking about, Kate? I'm done with trying to decode what you're saying. Just spit it out like an adult."

The fury in her eyes clouded over with pain, causing another aching strike to his chest. If he wasn't already pushed to the brink, he would have been more patient with her. The problem was they didn't have much time. She needed to start talking. Now.

"You're a cheater," she spat.

He released her wrist like it had burned him, and his mouth dropped open. "What did you just say?"

Her chin lifted, and the confidence returned to her eyes. "Who's *Rebecca*, Liam? Why don't you tell me all about the girl you're currently dating? *Then* try to explain why you had to keep her a secret from me."

Liam's eyes searched the ground as if he'd be able to make sense of the direction this conversation had taken. "Rebecc—" His gaze shot up to meet hers. "How do you know about Rebecca?"

"So, you're not denying it." She let out a sharp laugh. "That's just perfect."

He stepped toward her again. "Kate, how do you know about Rebecca?"

A flicker of fear filled her gaze but disappeared just as quickly. "I saw a message on your phone last night."

His brows lowered. "You went through my phone?"

Her eyes widened. "What? No! Of course not. But if you're trying to hide a girlfriend, maybe you should change your settings to make the messages that fill your screen *private*." Her voice had turned venomous. "Karma is a funny thing, Liam. It always comes full circle." She stumbled back a few steps until her hands reached the handle on the door. "You should go."

"You don't even want an explanation?" For all the pain and grief that had filled his body moments ago, his chest suddenly felt hollow. So this was how it would end. She'd kick him out of her life without giving him a chance to plead his case.

Her hard gaze confirmed everything running through his mind. Clenching his jaw tightly, he brushed past her and out into the empty hallway. So much for thinking he might have a second chance at finding love. He'd been fortunate enough to find it with Sarah. He'd been a fool to think luck would smile on him and bring him Kate too.

Chapter Twenty-One

Kate hugged her midsection. Though she'd managed to catch a late flight, her heart still seemed to be suffering the effects of her final encounter with Liam. Every few minutes, the burning sensation returned behind her eyes, making it hard to focus on anything she held in front of her.

The plane was mostly empty. That figured. People didn't tend to seek out flights that would get them in late at night. Christmas was three weeks away. This was likely a lull in the month right before people started their holiday travels.

A couple cuddled in their seats across the aisle from her, so caught up in their own little world, they probably didn't notice anyone was nearby, let alone on the plane. A twinge of envy replaced the ache in her chest. That could have been her. She'd managed to fall in love with two men, and both had slipped through her fingers.

Kate studied the girl a little closer. What was so great about her that she was able to find her perfect match? Sure, she was pretty, but not exceptionally so. Maybe she had a bubbly personality. Or maybe she was really smart.

A sigh left Kate's lips, and she settled back in her seat and looked out the window. She couldn't see anything. It was too dark for that, but it beat staring at the one thing she wished she could have.

Had everything worked out between her and Liam, she might have been able to sit by him and hold his hand on the way back to Maine. They could put their heads together and laugh while they people-watched on the plane or at the airport.

No. She shoved the thought aside. There would be no thinking about that lying jerk. He didn't deserve to have anyone think about him. A tear escaped, dragging in a line down her cheek. Nor did he deserve any tears to be shed over him. She wiped the salty water from her cheek with the heel of her hand and let out a shuddering breath.

It was like Ansley said: men weren't worth it. They couldn't be trusted. Men were only good for one thing—a fun night out.

The problem with that outlook was that Kate didn't want just one fun night after another. She wanted someone she could come home to. She wanted a partner she could trust.

Swallowing down the whimper that threatened to escape, Kate squeezed her eyes shut and focused on her breathing. She'd get in at around two in the morning, and she could just go to sleep.

Time. That was all that would help her get through this.

Chapter Twenty-Two

Liam held his champagne glass in his hand and swirled the bubbly, golden liquid. Each time a woman entered the ballroom, his attention shifted to the door. And each time he realized it wasn't Kate, his heart died a little more.

He shouldn't be surprised. Kate had skipped out on the last few competitions. They'd probably won three quarters of the events, but their fight had been enough to make her want to disappear.

What he really should do was march up to her room and force her to talk to him. But something told him she wouldn't be thrilled with that. It was more than just her accusations; it was the look of pain he read in her eyes. She needed to cool off. Then *if* she was ready to revisit a possibility with him, she'd have to make the first steps. Besides, tonight was the meteor shower. It was the whole reason he'd come. In about thirty minutes, he'd move out onto the balcony and enjoy the glitter flying through the sky in memory of Sarah.

A couple passed by him, smiling broadly. Several of the participants for the week seemed to remember him from the karaoke night. A few of the women had already inquired about Kate. All he could say was that she wasn't feeling well.

Liam couldn't help going over and over the way things had ended the night they'd gone to dinner. Something told him that was where everything had gone wrong. It wasn't the message from Rebecca, not really. It was that he'd allowed her to stew over the message and come to the worst possible conclusion. He shoved aside those thoughts, forcing himself to focus on why he was here.

Inevitably, he lost control anyway, coming right back to Kate and where things had gone wrong. The most terrible part was that he couldn't blame her. The one person she was supposed to be able to trust had lied to her. That sort of hurt sliced deep. If he were honest with himself, he'd admit that he'd be lucky to get her to talk to him again. There was only a slim chance she'd even be willing to hear him out when it came to who Rebecca was.

Liam let out a sigh and surveyed the room once more. The smart thing to do would be to cut his losses.

His phone buzzed in his pocket. He should probably ignore that too. His phone had only gotten him in more and more trouble. Liam let it ring through until it stopped. He took a sip of his beverage as he hovered near the wall and watched happy couples dance to "Baby, It's Cold Outside."

Pain sliced through his chest so suddenly, he sucked in a sharp breath. It was *her* song. The song that single-handedly made him start to fall for her. It all came back in one gut-wrenching string of memories. The way her eyes lit up when she was excited *or* upset. The way her voice sounded when she sang a song she loved. Even the way her smile made his heart melt and his knees go weak.

Emotion blurred his vision, and he spun around to place his champagne flute on the nearest table. He needed to talk to her before they left and never saw each other again. Sarah had wanted him to come here for a reason. She may not have known whether or not he'd follow through. Nor would she have been aware that coming would help him find love again. But the world worked in mysterious ways, and he'd be darned if he let another woman walk out of his life for a second time.

He was looking at this all wrong. It wasn't the meteor shower that was important. It was what the shower represented. Hope. If Sarah were here right now in this very moment, she'd be kicking him out the door and ordering him to go after what made him happy.

Kate made him happy.

Liam strode toward the elevators. His foot tapped as he waited for the contraption to come to a stop on his floor. The second the doors slid open, he burst between them, startling a couple about to exit.

Muttering an apology, he pushed the button for Kate's floor. Why couldn't the elevator go any faster? His foot continued its impatient tapping until the metal box lurched to a stop. He darted out into the foyer, sprinted down the hall, and skidded to a stop in front of her room.

His mouth hung open as he took in the open doorway and the maid cart sitting just outside her door. Liam peered into the room. Maybe she just needed someone to clean something up.

But even as the thought crossed his mind, he knew that wasn't the case. She was due to check out in the morning anyway.

The bed had been stripped of its linens. Two women spoke happily as one made the bed with fresh sheets and a comforter and the other wiped down the desk. The latter froze as she made eye contact with Liam. "Can I help you, sir?"

He shook his head and took a step back. Then thinking better of it, he nodded, clearing his throat. "Yes, actually. The woman who was staying here. Did she check out?"

The maids exchanged concerned glances. "We're not allowed to share that information with you. But if you want, you can head down to the front desk. They might be able to help."

Liam pressed his lips together into a firm line and gave them a sharp shake of his head. "Thanks, anyway."

It was almost like his feet couldn't bear to walk down the hallway, his shoes shuffling against the commercial-grade carpeting. His phone buzzed again, and he groaned. "Why won't anyone leave me alone?" He yanked his phone from his pocket just as a text from Rebecca came through. He'd already messaged her to cancel any future dates. His heart just wasn't in it.

Without reading the text, he opened his messaging app, intent on informing Tyson that there would be no more setups. Period. But a strange number hovered near the top of the screen. It was one he didn't recognize. His finger hovered over the message, then with a tap, he opened it. The image of a lit Christmas tree in all its glory filled the small screen. Under the image were the words "For inspiration–K."

His brows furrowed as he stared at the image. Then everything came together. Kate had sent this message to her friend. His eyes widened, and a smile spread across his face. Kate might not be willing to talk to him, but he had the next best thing.

Chapter Twenty-Three

Christmas Eve

"Okay. Explain to me again *why* you won't call him? It's been three weeks. Surely you're not going to just leave things the way they are." Ansley was draped over the love seat in Kate's apartment living room. She was scrolling through her phone, not even looking in Kate's direction.

Kate rolled her eyes as she added a few more sprinkles to the cookies she'd made for her neighbors. "I'm not going over this again with you. Honestly, Ansley, I don't understand why you're so obsessed with him."

Ansley's gaze darted to meet Kate's, and she lifted a shoulder in a half-hearted shrug. "I don't know. I just figured you sounded so happy when you were spending time with him at that resort."

Chest tight, Kate swallowed the lump in her throat. "I *was* happy, until I realized he's just like the rest of them. He's a liar who's only interested in what makes *him* happy."

"Sheesh, Kate. I didn't realize you turned into such a cynic."

Kate flinched as she went over what she'd just said in her

head. Ansley was right. Over the last three weeks, her attitude had continued to spiral. She'd fixated on everything that had developed between herself and Liam. Doing so had forced her heart into a constant state of unrest. Had she done the right thing? Should she have listened to him? Maybe, but he could have just as easily made the first step in mending bridges. It wouldn't have been that hard to track down her number.

"You okay?"

Kate jumped and stared at her friend. Concern was etched into Ansley's perfect features.

"Because you look like you want to murder that cookie." Ansley sat up and peered over at the counter. "What did that cute little Christmas tree ever do to you?" She made a poor attempt at hiding the amusement regarding her own statement.

Glancing down at the cookie, Kate groaned. Rather than being adorned with perfectly piped frosting like all the other cookies, the one in front of her looked like it had been done by a two-year-old. She opened the cupboard where the garbage can was and picked up the cookie.

"Don't you dare!" Ansley jumped off the love seat and scurried over to the island. She snatched the cookie out of Kate's hand and brought it to her lips with a flourish. "Mmm." She smiled before propping herself onto a bar stool and gave Kate a pointed look. "What if you were wrong?"

"Wrong about what?" Kate leaned over the next cookie, frosting bag poised.

"About Liam."

She flinched again. "I'm not."

"But what if you were?" Ansley pressed. "What if Liam was innocent and you walked away from the best person you ever had a chance to be with?"

Kate brought up her gaze to meet Ansley's. "Who are you, and what have you done with my best friend?"

Ansley gasped and placed a manicured hand on her chest. "I can be a romantic if the timing is right." She took another bite of her cookie. "Humor me. What if you were wrong and Liam was actually perfect for you? What would you do?"

One of Kate's brows arched as she studied her friend. "Nothing."

"Nothing?"

"That's right. Nothing. First of all, I don't have his number. Second of all, I *did* make a pretty big fool of myself. There's no coming back from that. Third—"

"You love him."

Kate choked on a bit of spittle when she sucked in a breath. The cough that followed was just as painful. "*What?*" she managed to spit out as soon as she caught her breath.

"You heard me. I've seen you in love, Kate. I know the signs. That means when you fell in love for a second time, it was like déjà vu. You are in love with that man, and you need to get him back."

A snort escaped Kate's lips. "I can't get him back."

"But you would if you could?"

Kate sighed, putting down her frosting bag. "I don't *know*." She glanced at Ansley, and her friend's wide eyes were drilling into her. "Okay, fine. *If* I found out I was wrong, *and* he wanted me back, sure, I'd try again. But none of that matters, because it's *never* going to happen."

Ansley tapped her finger on the counter, not speaking for a few minutes. "You know what we should do tonight?" Without waiting for a response, Ansley leaned forward and smiled brightly at her. "Karaoke."

Kate let out an exaggerated groan. "I don't want to go to a karaoke bar with you tonight. It's Christmas Eve, for heaven's sake. I bet there isn't even one open."

"I know of one."

Her brows creased. "Who would be crazy enough to have karaoke night on Christmas Eve?"

"Mulligan's."

Kate considered her friend for a few moments. Mulligan's *would* be the one place that would try to bring in some people before the festivities began tomorrow.

"You know you *want* to," Ansley sang. "And I'm sure they'll *only* be playing Christmas music. We could go, sing some songs, eat some junk food, and call it a night."

The offer *was* tempting. She could use an opportunity to burn off a little steam. The tension left her shoulders as she let them drop and allowed a smile to fill her face. "Okay. Let's do it."

Chapter Twenty-Four

Liam tapped his feet as he sat in his car, staring at Mulligan's. For a holiday—or the day before a holiday—the place was packed. It had just started snowing, and the flakes that landed on his front window melted immediately. He hadn't seen Kate arrive with her friend yet. At this point, Ansley hadn't confirmed that she'd been able to convince Kate to come tonight. This whole plan hinged on her making that happen.

His legs continued to bounce with anticipation. Three weeks felt like such a long time, and yet he knew the moment he saw her, it would be like no time had passed.

Liam grabbed his phone and pulled up his messages again. The last one he received from Ansley insisted she'd get Kate to karaoke, and he just had to arrive by eight. His focus shifted to the clock in the upper-right corner. It was five after the hour. If everything had gone according to plan, they would be inside the building right now.

This was his chance—possibly even the only moment he had to win her back. If he didn't convince her to hear him out, chances were high that she'd either leave or demand for him to do so. His heart pounded, and his hands grew clammy. Liam wiped them on his jeans then pulled his key from the ignition and climbed out of the car. He headed toward the front door and slipped inside.

"Jingle Bell Rock" played from the speakers while a group of guys sang their rendition of the song on the small stage at the far end of the space. The place smelled more like a bakery than a restaurant, like the menu only contained sweets for the night. The air hummed as groups of people chatted with one another.

Liam ducked through the crowd of people near the entrance, dodging out of the way of those on their way out. He slowed and let his gaze trail over the sea of faces. The one person he wanted desperately to find was nowhere to be seen. He should have messaged Ansley and requested an update. He pulled out his phone, planning to do just that.

The song ended, and the announcer jogged up to the stage. "All right, folks, give it up for Kate!" He applauded, stepping to the side of a familiar brunette wearing a crimson-red dress that swirled just below her knees. The hammering in Liam's chest intensified, and he froze, the phone in his hand forgotten.

Somewhere in the crowd, a woman screamed. "Woot! Go Kate!"

Kate laughed and shook her head as she grabbed the microphone from the stand and held it to her lips. She nodded to the guy manning the karaoke machine, and the music started up again. As if against his will, Liam's feet took off toward the stage. He skulked around the side, miraculously avoiding being seen by Kate, and made it to the guy at the equipment before the lyrics appeared on the little screen. "Change the song," he demanded.

The man stared at him, baffled. "What?"

"I said we're changing the song, buddy. Start this one." He jabbed his finger at the paper within a plastic sheet protector.

"But she didn't request—"

"Just do it."

The man shrugged, and within seconds, the music was shut off only to have a new song start. Kate shot a confused look at the man working the equipment just as "Baby, It's Cold Outside" started to play. Liam grabbed a secondary microphone and made his way up the steps.

Kate's mouth dropped open, causing her to miss her opening line.

His lips twitched into a smile as he brought the microphone toward them. He sang the first line then raised his eyebrows suggestively. "Come on, you know you want to join in," he murmured to the side.

She blinked, and he wandered around her, singing her next line, followed quickly by his own. She was clearly shocked to see him. By the time she was supposed to sing her third line, she'd recovered. Her voice was rich with color and sent chills down his spine.

The crowd let out a cheer. Liam laughed as he continued singing. Kate's eyes were alight with energy and the joy he'd fallen in love with when they'd been at the resort. Her voice wrapped around him like she was giving him a hug. This hadn't been the plan, but it had worked out better than anything he could have dreamed or rehearsed.

And just like that, it ended too soon. When the final line was sung in unison, everyone in the room stood on their feet and applauded. It took less than three minutes, and now he had one shot at explaining himself.

Kate hurried off the stage, leaving her microphone at the table, where a new couple were pointing out the song they wanted to sing. Liam hurried after her, shoving his microphone at the gentleman as he passed.

Flashes of her red dress was all he could see as Kate slipped through the crowd of people. At one point, he had to jump out of the way of a waitress while he chased Kate down. Where was she going? This wasn't how any of this was supposed to go.

She slipped through the entrance, but he was close behind. When he burst through the doors, he found her standing in the middle of a snowstorm. White flecks clung to her hair, giving her the appearance of a sugar plum fairy. Kate spun around to face him, her cheeks almost a near match to her dress.

"What are you doing here, Liam?" she asked breathlessly. "How did you know I was here?" There was that familiar pain in her gaze, the one he'd seen in their last moments together. It was almost like she was holding back her emotions, refusing to let him see her weakness.

He didn't move toward her for fear that she'd bolt if he did. Liam tried to swallow the lump in his throat, but it refused to budge. He bounced his fist against his leg and glanced back toward Mulligan's for just a moment before setting his gaze on Kate once more. "I begged Ansley to help."

Her brows shot up, and she let out a sharp laugh. "You're kidding."

Slowly, he wagged his head back and forth.

"Ansley isn't some hopeless romantic. What did you do to convince her? In fact, I could have sworn she disapproved of you more than I did. Did you pay her off or something?"

"What? No. I told her the truth." He took a step toward her. "I told her I was madly in love with her best friend."

"You—wait. You're—" she stammered.

"Madly, deeply, ardently"—he took another tentative step toward her—"in love with you." Liam was quickly closing the distance between them. "Back at the resort, you got it all wrong."

Skepticism still filled her eyes. "I saw the message, Liam. You didn't deny it. There was someone else."

He shook his head. "I've never met Rebecca. My buddy was attempting to set me up with her after I got back from the resort. I had zero interest in it from the start."

Her eyes widened. He couldn't dare hope that it would be this easy.

"In fact, we sort of talked about it at one point—our friends pushing us to do things we weren't thrilled about doing to begin with." He tilted his head and offered her a smile.

"I remember," she whispered.

A thrill exploded within him. This was working. Her gaze had shifted, softened somehow. He continued, "I came tonight because I knew I would never forgive myself if I didn't make this right—if I couldn't win you back." His voice lowered. "Because if there's one thing I've realized over the last few weeks, it's that I can't live without *you*, Kate. You've been the brightest thing in my life since I lost Sarah, and I was an idiot for letting you leave the way you did."

He stood in front of her now, under the moon and the falling snow. Reaching out, he hooked his finger under her chin. "There is no one else for me but you." He searched her eyes, searching for one thing. Finding it, he leaned down and brushed his lips against hers.

Sparks exploded behind his eyes, and he allowed them to close as she slipped her arms around his neck. He shifted, slipping his free hand around her waist, and pulled her tight against him. The crisp, cold air around them faded away, and fire ignited in his stomach and moved to his chest.

She slipped her fingers into the hair at the nape of his neck, eliciting a groan from his lips as they continued to rove against hers. This was everything his heart had needed, and it was even better knowing she wanted him like he wanted her.

Their kiss, tender and sweet, was the perfect way to seal what could be a future together.

She sucked in a shuddering breath before pulling back. "Oh, Liam..." Her mouth curved into a soft smile, and she placed her hands on either side of his face. "You have just given me the perfect Christmas present."

"Really?" His warm breath expelled a small puff into the cold air. His lips quirked into a half smile. "What's that?"

"You."

Epilogue

One Year Later

Kate entered the resort and immediately ran her mittened hands over her dripping hair, shaking loose the melted snow that clung to each wayward strand. She stomped her boots a few times then scanned the room until she met his eyes.

Those pine-green windows to his soul that could steal her breath away and make her heart pound faster than the hooves of a racing horse locked on to hers. Liam smiled at her, his gaze not leaving her face as she made her way toward him. This was what happiness felt like. True, unadulterated joy. These days, she wanted for nothing, because her heart was full. She had the love of a good man.

"How was the venue?" Liam put down his magazine on the table beside his chair. He reached forward, slipped his arms around her waist, and pulled her onto his lap.

She let out a breathless laugh but still threw her arms around his neck. "*Liam*! I'm dripping wet! It's nearly a blizzard out there."

He craned his head around her, looking out the large glass

windows of the doors on the far side of the lobby. "I *told* you we should have had a June wedding, but you insisted."

Kate laughed again, slipping her hands into the hair at the back of his head. "Don't you pin this on me. It was *you* who wanted to come all the way out here to get married. The problem with *that* is we can't control the weather." She glanced over her shoulder toward the doors herself. "I doubt we'll be able to get any good outdoor pictures or be able to do any of the activities we planned. The forecast says it might even get worse."

Liam reached up and grasped her chin with his finger and thumb. "Hey, it's okay. I don't need any of that. I just need you." He kissed the tip of her nose. "That's all I'll ever need."

"And tomorrow, when we stand in front of our family and friends, you will get exactly that." Kate leaned down, claiming his mouth with hers. "One more day," she murmured as she pulled back. "And I'm all yours."

"Ack. Get a room, you two."

Kate pulled back and giggled as she met Ansley's gaze. It was a blend of amusement and something else she couldn't put her finger on. Her friend placed her hands on her hips and shook her head, letting out an exaggerated groan and causing several heads to turn their way. "You guys are lucky I think you're so cute together. Or this would have never happened." She gestured to the two of them before she wandered off, leaving a trail of wet snow in her wake as it fell from her boots and coat.

"She's right, you know," Liam murmured, his gaze following Ansley until she disappeared from view. "If she hadn't been willing to help me win you back, this wedding might not have even happened. I'm still surprised she didn't block my number."

Kate nodded. "Yeah, I know." Ansley had surprised them both.

"Maybe we should do something for her—you know, to show her our appreciation."

She met Liam's gaze once more. "Like what? A necklace?"

He chuckled, tucking a wet strand of hair behind her ear as he shook his head. "Naw, I'm thinking something—bigger. You know, more *romantic*."

Her brows furrowed, and she tilted her head. "I know that look. Liam Harper, what are you planning?"

Her fiancé shrugged, but his smile widened further, making her heart skip a beat.

He shifted and looked away for just a moment. "I don't know if you'd approve."

Kate leaned back, studying him. Her eyes narrowed, and she pressed her lips into a thin line. This was Liam she was talking to. He was a big ol' romantic at heart. If anyone could help Ansley in that department, it was him. "You know what? I trust you. Whatever it is, I'm game."

A deep chuckle escaped his chest, vibrating through her body. "Good. Because I already invited someone to the wedding who I think is perfect for her, and I fully intend on making them fall in love while we're at the resort." He gestured around them at the high ceilings, the Christmas decor, and the mistletoe that hung over the fireplace in the corner. "This place helped *us* fall in love, why can't it work for Ansley too?"

Warmth spread throughout her entire body, and a mischievous smile filled her face. He made a good point. "I'm so in."

Liam pulled her in for one more deep, toe-curling kiss before he pulled back again, leaving Kate somewhat dazed. He brushed his thumb along her jaw and set those heart-stopping eyes on her. "I knew there was a reason I fell in love with you."

Come Back to Sweet Paradise Resort

Grab another cup of hot chocolate and cozy up with the next Sweet Paradise Resort holiday romance.

Weddings are difficult...even without the maid of honor and best man being at odds.

Ansley doesn't believe in love.

Her best friend is heading down the aisle for a second time, and she hopes this union will go better than the first. There's nothing she wouldn't do for Kate, including being her maid of honor. There's only one problem: the best man couldn't be more stuck up if he tried.

Zane has a two-date rule, which makes his love life less complicated.

People are fickle, and he'd rather not get attached to anyone who could eventually leave him. But then Ansley enters his life, and suddenly, he's second-guessing his decision to keep his distance.

As Ansley's wedding duties continue to mount, she has no choice but to accept Zane's help.

But when the two join forces to give their best friends the perfect ceremony, will they stumble upon a romantic connection that could change everything they thought they knew about love?

Merry Mistletoe Wedding is available for purchase at www.hopeaugust.com and select book retailers.

Paperback, large print, and book bundles are available at www.hopeaugust.com

Also by Hope August

Sweet Paradise Resort Christmas

Saving Paradise Resort (series prequel)

Merry Mistletoe Wedding

Christmas Cookies and Coworkers

Maid for Mistletoe Mix-up

A Sweet Paradise Holiday Reunion

Sagebrush Dude Ranch Christmas

Snowfall Over Sagebrush (series prequel)

Mistletoe Masquerade

Gingerbread Hearts

Beneath the Christmas Star

Tinsel Trail

Crossroads at Sagebrush

Visit www.hopeaugust.com to purchase these and other new releases by Hope August.

About the Author

Hope August lives in central Texas with her family, which includes two chihuahua mix rescues. She loves reading romance stories with all the feels and creating characters you might recognize in real-life.

One more thing...

If you enjoyed this story, please consider sharing your thoughts with other readers so they can enjoy it, too. Leave an honest review at www.hopeaugust.com or anywhere this book is sold.

Thank you!

BB bookbub.com/authors/hope-august

www.ingramcontent.com/pod-product-compliance
Lightning Source LLC
Chambersburg PA
CBHW052206170626
46812CB00004B/1681